laptop #5

dangerous encounters

Tangled Truths & Twisted Tales—Exposed!

by Christopher P.N. Maselli

Zonder**kidz**

To Kim Culp, whose constant prayers for this series haven't gone unnoticed.

Zonder**kidz**.

The children's group of Zondervan

www.zonderkidz.com

Dangerous Encounters
Copyright © 2003 by Christopher P. N. Maselli

Requests for information should be addressed to:
Grand Rapids, Michigan 49530

ISBN: 0-310-70664-5

Editor: Gwen Ellis

Interior Design: Beth Shagene & Todd Sprague

Art Direction: Jody Langley

Printed in the United States of America

03 04 05 /❖DC/ 5 4 3 2 1

Contents

Contents

The inventor knew he had misjudged them, but by the time he realized it, it was too late. He was forced to disappear—lose his life—in hopes that one day he might find it again. When he vanished, they thought they had won. They thought he was dead. Little did they know, they had misjudged him.

"Go! Go! Go!" Gill thumped the back of his dad's leather seat as if it were a bongo drum.

"Yes! Go!" Mrs. Gillespie shouted at her husband. Her head was pressed back against the headrest, her hands were wrapped around her stomach.

"I'm going! I'm going!" Gill's dad, Jason Gillespie, yelled back.

The Security Bank security truck screeched its wheels as it tore out of the driveway. Matt Calahan, sitting beside Gill in the backseat, buckled his seat belt as fast as he could. He looked out the window, feeling oddly like a criminal locked in the back of a police car. He popped open his laptop and waited for it to boot.

"Where were you, Gill?" Jason Gillespie asked as he propelled the truck down Oleander Street, picking up speed with each roar of the engine. "Didn't your beeper go off?"

"Yes!" his red-headed son shouted. "And it *kept* going off! I told you it tickles me when it vibrates. I couldn't stop laughing long enough to get over here! Besides, I wanted to get Matt!"

Matt dropped his head. "Thanks, Gill," he whispered. *As if* it were *his* fault they were late. He didn't really want to go, anyway, but Gill had insisted, as he had all *three* times they'd rushed to the hospital so far. They had all been false alarms. Gill's parents were way too excited about having a baby, and every time Mrs. Gillespie felt uncomfortable—whoosh!— off to the hospital.

Gill, on the other hand, wasn't so thrilled about his soon-to-be sibling. Matt didn't know *why* Gill didn't want a little brother or sister, but he knew he needed to stick by his friend. In some way, Matt felt responsible for Gill. He just might be the only person who could help Gill . . . with a keystroke or two.

Matt's laptop was fully booted. He placed his fingers on his keyboard, ready to assist as needed. Ironically, Gill's parents never did ask why Matt always had to come along. Nor did they seem to wonder why Matt was always typing. They must have figured he was just one of Gill's best friends, documenting the event. Or then again, maybe they were just preoccupied. Little did they know, Matt's laptop was no ordinary laptop. Little did they know that whatever Matt typed into the laptop actually *happened*—all he had to do was press the key with the clock face. Then the laptop went into action. Matt didn't understand *how* it worked, but it did. And at times like this, Matt was thankful that he had it. Other times, though ...

"Type, Matt!" Gill ordered in a harsh whisper.

Matt ran his hand through his black hair. He leaned toward the center of the car and peered out the front window. He saw the stoplight turn red. Quickly he typed,

> Immediately the stoplight at the crossing of Stewart and Reed turned green.

He hit the clock key. The on-screen arrow cursor turned into a golden analog clock, swiftly ticking forward. A second later it stopped and Matt looked up.

The stoplight instantly turned green. A white pickup and a green VW Bug came to a screeching halt, the rears of the vehicles popping into the air.

"Aaaaggghhhh!" Mrs. Gillespie screamed.

"Whoo-hoo!" Gill cheered as they sailed through the intersection.

"Sweet," Mr. Gillespie said.

Matt cracked a smile.

"We'll be there in no time," Gill's dad said, trying to comfort his wife.

"We'd better!" she shouted, her fingernails digging into the soft roof. "Or next time *you're* having the baby!"

Matt watched Mr. Gillespie stomp on the gas pedal.

"Oh no!" Gill pointed forward. "There's a dump truck blocking the street!"

Mr. Gillespie now stomped on the brake pedal.

"You're slowing down!" Gill's mom complained, her auburn hair spreading out on her headrest like a squashed starfish.

"What am I supposed to do? Plow through it?"

Matt furiously typed. "Take Henson Boulevard," he stated matter-of-factly. "It'll be clear."

Mr. Gillespie turned onto Henson Boulevard, obeying without question, like a dazed clone.

"How do you know it'll be clear?" Gill asked Matt.

Matt turned the laptop so Gill could read the screen.

```
Henson Blvd was blocked to thru traffic
and free for Mr. Gillespie to drive down.
```

"Nice," Gill said.

As they shot down Henson Boulevard, they passed an intersection blocked by a tipped ice cream truck. Ice cream was spilled everywhere, holding up crossing traffic on the now-rocky road.

"Is that what you meant to do?" Gill asked, reading once again what Matt had typed.

Matt twisted his lip. "Hmm. No. But then again, sometimes the best stories thrive on misunderstandings."

"Cool—like sitcoms!"

Matt grimaced. *Leave it to Gill to relate literary prowess back to television.* "Yes, like sitcoms," he conceded.

"How much longer?" Mrs. Gillespie shouted, pounding the floorboard with her foot.

"Not long!" Gill's dad promised, cranking into another turn.

With the road clear, Matt relaxed and turned to Gill. "So you're about to be a big brother, eh?"

Gill rolled his eyes.

"What?"

"You know what," Gill retorted.

"I just want life to get back to normal."

Matt chuckled. "Normal life? You mean the normal life where Hulk Hooligan is still upset at you for upchucking all over him?"

Gill waved a hand. "Actually he hasn't bothered me at all." Then he added, "Speaking of normal life, is Isabel still mad at you for sabotaging your date?"

"It wasn't a date, it was a youth function," Matt insisted. "But yes. Alfonzo told me she couldn't get the chocolate cake out of her dress."

Gill's eyebrows perked up. "I didn't know chocolate-cake-slinging was involved."

"Trust me, you don't want to know. Besides, chocolate cake is the least of my worries. For all I know, Sam's going to show up again and try to rope me into something. Fat chance."

Gill shuddered. "I hope he doesn't show up again."

Matt knew. Gill didn't like Sam because Gill wasn't fond of danger. And Sam, the previous owner of Matt's amazing laptop, *reeked* of danger. It was only recently that Matt had discovered that the mysterious man was even alive . . . and ready to meddle in Matt's laptop business.

"We can't be afraid of him," Matt said. "That's what he wants."

"Easier said than done."

"Tell me about it."

Whoooooooooooooooooooo!

Matt, Gill, and Gill's mom all shifted around and looked out the back window. Mr. Gillespie peered into the rearview mirror. His shoulders dropped.

"We're being pulled over," he stated.

"I can see that, but you can't stop!" Gill's mom protested.

"I can't *not* stop!" he replied.

A moment later the security vehicle was idling by the curb as a female police officer stepped off her motorcycle. She slowly strolled to the driver's side window as Mr. Gillespie rolled it down.

Matt typed,

> Mrs. Gillespie makes it to the hospital with flying colors.

"License and reg—," the officer began, then she said, "Hey, is that you, Jason?"

Mr. Gillespie smiled. "Betty! Hi!" He turned to his wife. "Hey, Jill, this is Betty. We worked together sometimes when I was on the force."

Mrs. Gillespie had a pinched look on her face and seemed to be forcing her smile. "Jason . . ."

"Oh, right! Say, Betty, I'm sorry we were speeding, but my wife's having a baby, and—"

"A baby! Oh! Say no more. Been there, done that! Turn on your lights—I'll escort you."

"Right!"

Officer Betty ran back to her motorcycle and pulled out, her lights twirling, her siren blaring. Mr.

Gillespie flipped on the top lights of his security vehicle and pulled in behind her.

"Cool!" Gill shouted.

The motorcycle-truck caravan raced down the road, parting traffic like Moses parted the Red Sea, but without all the water mess.

"I'm so embarrassed!" Gill's mom lamented.

As they flew down the road, Gill peeled his eyes away from the flashing red and white of the police cycle just long enough to glance at Matt's laptop. "Flying colors," he said.

Matt smiled. "Not what I meant, but see, sometimes misunderstandings aren't so bad!"

Gill playfully socked Matt in the shoulder. "Man, you couldn't top this!"

Matt nodded. "Let's hope I don't have to."

Matt, Gill, Lamar, and Alfonzo—the QoolQuad, as they called themselves—were biking up and down Oleander Street, in front of their homes. Matt's house was in the center of the block, a two-story, wooden, musty–white house with black trim.

Across the street was Alfonzo's house, a huge three-story mansion that even had a basement. Outside, ivy eerily snaked up the brick. The creaky old gate was one of the first things Mr. Zarza had removed when they moved up from Mexico. Matt was thankful they were remodeling the house so fast—it had been a real eyesore for years.

Gill's house was next to Matt's. It was an odd turquoise color that somehow worked in the neighborhood. It was just one story, with a small yard and an always open garage.

Lamar's house, where Matt had spent many hours, was a few doors down, on the other side. It was brick red and white with plenty of lush, dark green bushes out front. A long, stark-black Cadillac sat in the driveway now. Oscar, the man Lamar's mom had started dating, was visiting again ... which was probably the reason Lamar was the first one outside on his bike.

"I can't believe it was *another* false alarm," Lamar said.

"I'll believe it's over when I see the baby," Matt said flatly.

Gill shivered as if Matt had just made his skin crawl. "My parents are way too nervous. The doctor says it's like ... hiccups or something."

"Hiccups don't do that to me."

"Well, they sure do it to my mom. I'm telling you, that thing is *trouble*."

Matt winced. "It's not a *thing*, Gill. It's not even an *it*. It's your baby brother or sister. Are you sure you're not just scared about being a big brother?"

"I'm not scared," Gill scoffed. "I don't scare easily."

"Look! There's Sam!" Matt yelled.

Gill ducked. "Where?"

The boys laughed.

Alfonzo had constructed a small ramp out of wooden planks. Gill shot over it, his bicycle launching into the air and landing with a thump.

"Personally," Gill added as he spun around, "I'm glad I'm not a girl. Because who wants to have babies?" He shuddered. "Not me. I'll adopt. Just like my parents adopted me. But no, they had to go the extra mile and have one themselves."

"Yeah," Alfonzo offered as he kicked up his speed. "But you're just playin', right? I mean, you want another Gillespie, don't you?" Pow! He shot over the ramp and then screeched to a halt.

 Gill waited for Alfonzo to turn around. "Well, it's not even born yet and look how much trouble it's been! Demanding all that attention. Giving my mother bad hiccups."

"So is it a boy or a girl?" Alfonzo asked.

"We don't know. My parents want it to be a big surprise. I don't really care. They'll see soon enough that it's a monster."

"It's not so bad," Alfonzo said, assuring Gill. "I mean, Iz was a handful when she was born—still is. But don't knock being a big brother until you've tried it."

Matt squinted and stopped pedaling. "You weren't even *two* when Isabel was born. You can't remember that far back."

"Trust me. If you've ever heard my sister scream, you'd remember."

Matt conceded the point. He looked at Alfonzo's house, his eyes drawing across the structure until they settled on the window to Isabel's room on the second floor. He cleared his throat. "So, er, how is she?"

Alfonzo shot down the street and jumped off the ramp again before he answered. "Man, I don't know if she's upset or just working things out. But I warned you. I told you after our mom left that she didn't need her heart broken again."

Gill shook his head. "I heard about the chocolate-cake-slinging incident."

Suddenly the crew froze. They could nearly feel the ground shake as they watched the figure round the corner. It was the six-foot, two-hundred-and-some-pound bully of Enisburg Junior High in the flesh. With a frown on his face. *Hulk Hooligan.*

Gill gulped. "He's come to kill me," he whispered.

"Can you blame him? You puked on him—on *TV*," Alfonzo noted.

"Thanks for reminding me," Gill whimpered. "Just for that, upon my passing, Lamar gets my stereo instead of you."

"Hey!" Hulk roared as he drew close to their ramp.

Gill hopped off his bike, punched down the kick-stand, turned around, and opened his arms. "Okay, beat me up," he said to Hulk. "Do your worst. I deserve it. I'm tired of acting like the Road Runner trying to escape Wile E. I'm going to be a man and stand my ground."

"He gets kinda melodramatic when his life's on the line," Matt explained to Hulk.

"Kill ya?" Hulk shouted. "I'm not gonna kill ya! Whatdaya dink I am? A Neanderdal?"

Gill said, "Well, now that you mention it . . ."

Hulk sneered.

Gill put his arms down. "So you're not gonna kill me?"

"You kiddin'? Everywhere I go, kids want my autograph. Dey saw me skatin' and saw ya barf on me. On TV! Man, dey dought it was high-larious! I got carpo tunnel fer signin' so much!"

"This can't be happening," Gill whimpered.

"Ya rule, Gillespie! Jus' wanted ta say danks."

"Way to go, Gill," Matt said.

"Shuddup, Calhan," Hulk ordered.

"Cal-a-han," Matt corrected, pronouncing each syllable.

"Oh, by the way," Hulk added, leaning into Gill and holding a clenched fist between their faces, "don't let it happen again."

Gill gulped. Hulk walked away, the ground rumbling with each step. Gill waited until he was out of earshot, then said, "How come I was the star of the commercial and he's the one who became famous? Makes no sense."

"You know what doesn't make sense?" Lamar asked. His three friends turned to look at him.

"What?" Matt wondered aloud.

"My mom dating that loser." He straddled his bike, his head nodding toward the black Cadillac.

"Why don't you want your mom to date?" Matt asked. "I thought you were okay with this. It's been like fourteen years since your dad died, Lamar. I know she hasn't dated before, but c'mon. She's a grown woman."

"It's not that," Lamar said. "It's . . . I think this guy's bad news."

Matt let out a long breath. He flashed back to Lamar's uneasy feelings weeks ago at the winter banquet. He wasn't keen on his mother going out with Oscar then, and though Matt thought he'd come to accept it that night, obviously his concern had only grown. "What do you mean, 'bad news'?"

"I don't know. Like he's into something."

"Well, what do you mean, 'into something'? You mean something serious, like drugs—or just something weird, like pulling heads off Barbie dolls?"

"*That* would make Iz scream," Alfonzo said.

"I mean something serious," Lamar answered. "There's more to him than what he's letting on. I think he's holding a secret."

"Welcome to the club," Matt said.

"No, I mean a dangerous secret."

"Welcome to the club," Matt said again.

Gill prodded for more, "For instance . . ."

"Well, I've noticed he's always making phone calls and leaving abruptly."

Matt shrugged. "What's his job?"

Lamar's eyes darted back to the black Cadillac. "He says he's a loan officer."

"And you don't believe him?"

Now Lamar shrugged. "There's something else. I don't know what it is, but I'm telling you, he has a secret. I can feel it."

Matt pursed his lips. He knew Lamar well . . . and he knew his friend was probably just uncomfortable with someone dating his mother. Still, Matt hesitated to press the point.

"Well," Matt said, "I can't say. I've only met him that one time at the winter banquet, and I don't want to judge him without knowing."

Lamar looked at Matt. "Wanna come over?"

2

Skirting the Issues

So what's our plan?"

"Our plan?"

Matt nodded. "Yeah, our plan. We need a plan. We need to get to the truth and put this to rest once and for all."

"Yeah," Gill said to Lamar, "we need a plan to get to the truth. Don't you watch detective shows?"

"What kind of plan do we need?" Lamar asked.

"A good one," Gill said.

"Thanks for clearing that up." Lamar bit his lip. "Maybe Alfonzo had the right idea, staying outside and riding his bike. Maybe I should go back out and you guys can fill me in on what you learn."

Gill held up a finger. "See, if you watched detective shows, you'd realize that *that* would look suspicious."

Matt stood up and looked around Lamar's bedroom. The small area was covered floor to ceiling with posters, many of which Lamar himself had drawn. There were muscle-bound superheroes, penciled portraits, colorful comics, and many featured the characters Matt had worked into his stories over the years. Often, as Lamar sat on his bed and doodled, Matt sat at Lamar's wall desk, writing stories they brainstormed together. One day they would create a bestselling series. One superhero after another even swirled around Lamar's computer screen.

Gill rubbed his hands together. "Okay, so, you have any glasses in here?"

"I don't wear glasses."

"No, I mean drinking glasses," Gill said.

"There's a mug on my desk," Lamar pointed out.

Matt grabbed it and tossed it to Gill. "What do you have in mind?"

Gill inspected the mug and then pushed it against the door. He put his ear to the other end.

"What are you doing?" Matt asked.

"Listening."

After a few moments Lamar asked, "What do you hear?"

"Mostly 'mmmhmmmf, mmmhmmmf, mmmhmmmf.'" Gill set the mug down.

"This isn't helping," Matt said. "Why don't we just go out there and talk to them?"

"Because you can learn more by listening," Gill replied. "I read that in a Ziggy comic." He pulled the door open a little and peeked out through the crack.

Matt walked to the door. He pushed Gill down and peeked out above him. At the end of the hallway, which was lined with family pictures, he saw light coming from the kitchen.

Meow!

Matt and Gill looked down. Lamar's cat, Cuddles, peered up at them, her golden eyes expectant, her black tail straight up in the air, quivering.

"Shhh!" Lamar shushed Cuddles. He stood tiptoe behind Matt and Gill, looking out over Matt's head.

Meow!

"She's blowing our cover," Gill whispered.

Meow!

Lamar pushed Matt and Matt pushed Gill and the door slammed shut with a bang. Gill shoved his friends back and reopened the door. Cuddles was gone.

"There," Lamar said.

"You know what?" Gill offered. "I think you should just go out there and talk to them."

"Good idea," Matt said. "Good conversation is truly a blessing."

Gill looked at Matt, his eyebrow arched. "That's Ziggy, too."

Lamar pushed Matt and Gill aside. "Then let's get Ziggy with it." He exited the room and started down the hallway. Matt followed close behind him. At the end of the hallway Lamar stopped and turned. Matt looked back. Gill still stood in Lamar's bedroom.

"Aren't you coming?" Lamar asked him.

"I'll be your backup," Gill explained.

"What does that mean?"

"That means he's going to let us do the tough work," Matt interpreted, "while he plays video games."

Lamar nodded. "Good idea, Gill. You be our backup. Then later we can go to your house and you can teach us some more detective tips. You can even break out the *Blues Clues* videos and *I Spy* books."

Gill put his hands on his hips. "You mock me."

Lamar smiled.

When Matt and Lamar entered the kitchen, Matt saw Lamar's mom, Lorraine Whitmore, sitting at the table beside Oscar, a handsome black man with graying hair. Her round body was leaning in as she looked at a stack of pictures Oscar was thumbing through. The teacup in front of her had several bright red lipstick stains on the rim. She always wore bright red lipstick, thick and proud. She giggled, pointing to the next shot.

"My oh my, there's a keeper," she said.

Matt had a hard time believing Oscar was truly bad news. His parents always said that eventually

Lamar's mom would get married again. She was an attractive woman in her late thirties, with all the personality and fervor of a twenty-year old. Sooner or later it was bound to happen.

When she spotted the boys, she waved them over. "Hey, boys, c'mon and have a seat. You 'member Oscar from your date, Matt?"

"It was really just a youth function," Matt said, smiling at Oscar.

Oscar smiled back. "Nice to meet you again."

As Matt and Lamar took seats across the rectangular table, Matt glanced at Lamar and raised his eyebrows as if to say, "Hiding something? I highly doubt it."

Oscar set the pictures down on the table. Lamar pulled the stack toward himself. Using his index finger, he slid one after another off the stack.

His mom stood and made her way to the kitchen cupboards. "Didn't I hear Gill come in, too?" she asked.

Matt nodded. "He's backing up."

She started rummaging through one cupboard after another. "Oscar and I are going out to dinner tonight," she announced. "Lamar, I know there's some mac and cheese in here somewhere."

Matt nudged Lamar. "Can I stay for dinner?"

"You're welcome to if you want," Lamar's mom offered.

"My mom hasn't had time lately for real cooking," Matt explained.

Ms. Whitmore smiled and angled her head down at Lamar. "You'd better heat up some peas, too, boy."

"You guys have gone to a lot of places together," Lamar said, not looking up from the pictures.

"Been a lot of fun." Ms. Whitmore pulled out a box of EasyMac and set it on the counter.

"So I hear you are a writer, Matt," Oscar said.

Matt's eyes darted to Oscar. He wondered how he knew that. "Er ... yeah, I like to write."

"I once met a guy who liked to write. He is dead now, though. Unfortunate car accident."

Matt blinked.

"Lot of those going around ..."

Matt forced a little laugh. "Yeah." The reporter in him pressed in, changing the subject. "So, Oscar, I hear you're a loan officer."

The man smiled, his cheeks crinkling his brown eyes. "Yes, but I am hoping to retire."

Matt nodded. "Why is that?"

"It is a rough business. No one seems to like you much when you come after them for payments. That is the part of my job I do not like."

"Oh, so you don't give loans, you follow up on the people who don't pay?"

"Well, I do both. But if someone stops paying, I have to get tough." A long pause followed and then Oscar added, "But I am planning to get out of the business soon. If I can."

Lamar's mom chuckled. "Why couldn't you?"

"The family may not approve."

Matt gulped. Lamar looked up from the pictures.

"The f-f-family?" Lamar asked.

"Yes, well, you know families."

Matt and Lamar didn't take their eyes off him.

"Oh!" Lamar's mother walked toward the table, pointing to the next picture in the stack. "That's the beginning of the float your youth pastor is building for the annual parade."

The boys' eyes dropped to the picture. It showed a long, wide trailer with two wheels and a hitch. Chicken wire was bound to the top of it. Pastor Ruhlen, a lanky young man with yellow Chia Pet hair, smiled widely in the forefront.

"Yeah, he asked us to help him build it," Lamar said. Then he asked, "Ma, why do you have a picture of it in here?"

"Because Oscar bought it for him!" Ms. Whitmore beamed as she said it.

Oscar smiled. "It was the least I could do. The church needs a float."

"That must have been expensive," Matt noted.

"My family had the resources."

"You know it's a contest?" Ms. Whitmore asked her son.

"A contest?" Matt repeated.

"Yes. Every year the mayor judges the floats and one wins the prize."

"Wow," Matt said. "For best float?"

"Used to be for the best-*decorated* float," Oscar said. "But they felt it always went to whoever spent the most money. So this year they changed it. This year first place goes to 'Most Exciting Presentation.'"

"Which is why you need to help Pastor Ruhlen win," she added. She pulled out a couple plates.

Oscar shifted in his chair and adjusted his coat. As his jacket moved back, for a split second Matt saw the tip of something wide and shiny. He blinked and shook his head.

Lorraine Whitmore turned and set two napkins and two forks on the table.

Matt gulped. Oscar looked down at his jacket with a frown, then back up at Matt. He narrowed his eyes, clearly trying to read Matt, but Matt tried to keep his face blank.

Matt's gaze shifted to the photos of Lamar's mom and Oscar. Lamar was right, they did *everything* together. He let out a long breath. Something suspicious was happening, all right.

Lamar crashed onto his bed. "This is the end of my life."

"What?" Gill wondered. "What happened?"

Without saying a word, Matt plopped onto Lamar's desk chair.

"What!" Gill wanted to know.

"This guy is dangerous," Lamar exclaimed, "and he's got my mom wrapped around his finger!"

"Something is definitely off," Matt agreed. "You're right. He's not coming completely clean."

"He kept skirting the issues," Lamar said, jumping up from his bed.

"And he talked about 'the family' and 'unfortunate car accidents.' Lots of them."

"He *did*?" Gill cried.

Lamar buried his head in his hands. "This isn't happening!"

"And he never *once* used a contraction!" Matt noted.

Gill's face scrunched up.

"A contraction," Matt said. "You know, like *can't* and *don't* and *wasn't*. Something's not right about that." His eyes darted to Gill. Then he looked at

Lamar. "Guys, I think I saw something," he finally said.

Lamar and Gill looked at Matt.

"You can't freak out," Matt warned Lamar.

"What is it?"

"Sit down."

Lamar sat on the edge of his bed.

"Well," Matt continued slowly, "I think I'm wrong. I'm *sure* I'm wrong. But I think I saw a handle in his jacket pocket."

"A handle? To what?"

"A . . . gun?"

Lamar's jaw dropped. Gill covered his mouth.

"But I'm sure I'm wrong."

"No!" Gill exclaimed. "Matt, it makes total sense! 'Family'! *Unfortunate* accidents! You know what it sounds like to me? Organized crime."

"C'mon, Gill," Matt said. "You think he's a mobster?"

"Well, I don't think he's a loan officer."

Matt watched the heroes replace each other on the screen saver. Sometimes he wished he had muscles like that. Then he got an idea. "The Net. Let's check him out on the Net. Everything's on the Net."

Lamar hopped up and he and Gill leaned over Matt as he moved the mouse and stopped the screen saver. He clicked once, then twice, then started the Internet browser. A few moments later Lamar's computer had dialed in to his provider and was ready to go.

"What's his last name again?" Matt asked.

"Brown."

Matt went to a search engine and typed,

```
Oscar Brown
```

The search returned 1,289 hits.

"Great," Matt said.

He clicked the first one. The page came up, Sesame Street characters dancing around the borders. In the center an editorial read,

```
But if you ask me, that's the way it
should be. I mean, really, how realistic
is it that Oscar can litter anyway? So
what, he's a grouch! The show is totally
unrealistic. In the real world, he'd get
anywhere from a $500 fine to a year in
jail. IMO, Big Bird ought to nail his
can shut one night when the green and
brown Furby is sleeping. Furthermore . . .
```

"Hee hee. Furby," Gill said with a chuckle.

Matt hit the back arrow. "I don't think that helps." He selected five more hits, one after another, but came up with nothing but complete nonsense. Sesame Street characters and colors. That was it. "We're getting nowhere," he finally said.

"I gotta pray," Lamar whimpered.

Matt ran his hand through his hair. "I'm still not convinced. We need more evidence. We have to be smart about this. I mean, what do we really know about him?"

Click! The computer disconnected.

"Great!" Matt shouted, exasperated. "What's up with that?" He tried to reconnect twice more but nothing happened. He picked up the phone to check for a dial tone. Suddenly, he heard Oscar's voice on the line.

"Yes, tomorrow is good. Meet me after lunch. At the old school on the corner of Wesemann and Adams."

The voice on the other end cracked. "You mean the abandoned one? Isn't that a bit . . . desolate?"

"It is perfect," Oscar responded. "I have . . . access. You *will* be there, right?"

"Uh, yeah, whatever you say. You're the boss. I—"

Matt softly hung up the phone.

"What?" Lamar asked.

"You want to get to the bottom of this?" Matt asked.

Lamar nodded.

"Then let's follow him."

America's Most Dangerous

3

Y ou know," Alfonzo pointed out, "this isn't a great section of town."

"I know," Matt agreed. "I think that pawnshop where my dad got my laptop is around here somewhere."

Matt, Lamar, Gill, and Alfonzo hid their bikes behind a trash dumpster at the back of the old abandoned school on the corner of Wesemann and Adams. They had seen Oscar's black Cadillac out front, so they knew he had arrived. They had also spotted a small red automobile parked beside it. Gill identified it as a "cool Pinto." Matt told him that was an oxymoron.

The QoolQuad made their way around the side of the school. Matt felt as if he were walking through a ghost town. The basketball hoops were rusted, the jungle gym was peeling, and the cracked swings slowly swayed in the breeze. Lamar quietly tried to open a side door but it was locked. In fact, *every* door they tried was locked.

"Maybe he knows we're on to him," Gill suggested after the fifth try.

Matt shook his head. "There's nothing to be 'on to' yet . . . nothing concrete, anyway."

Alfonzo laughed nervously. "You said that he talked about his family like they were organized crime *and* that you know he's not telling the truth! That sounds pretty concrete to me. Whatever's up, he doesn't need to be dating Ms. Whitmore."

"I'm telling you," Lamar agreed, "every time I see him and my mom together, my stomach starts hurting. He's hiding something, I just know it."

Matt didn't respond. This wasn't the first time he had seen Lamar get nervous and jump to conclusions before he knew all the facts. Just a few weeks ago Lamar was sure that escorting Hulk's tattooed cousin, Nicki, to the winter banquet would be pure horror. In the end Lamar and Nicki were the ones who enjoyed themselves the most. Matt just wanted to make sure that Lamar's suspicions about Oscar were more than just a case of the nerves about his mother dating. Even if all the evidence *did* seem to indicate that something was wrong.

"So how are we gonna get in?" Lamar asked.

"We haven't tried all the doors yet, guys," Matt said, getting irritated. "There's still one that leads in through the greenhouse."

"Oh!" Gill exclaimed, as they walked toward the dome. "Speaking of bad guys, did you guys see *America's Most Dangerous* last night?"

Matt asked, "You watch that stuff?"

They reached the greenhouse and Matt tried the door.

Gill continued, "Yeah, so there's this guy and—"

"It's unlocked!" Matt exclaimed. The boys fell silent and looked at each other, not sure what they were about to find inside. The door opened with a creak, and one after another they entered the greenhouse. It smelled old and musty and moldy. Dirty brown circles spotted built-in ledges, like giant connect-the-dots. Matt squeezed his nose with his fingers.

At the other side of the room Matt grabbed a door-knob and slowly turned it. He peeked out but didn't see anyone or anything except an abandoned hall of dented lockers. He nodded to his friends, pulled the door fully open, and stepped out.

Cautiously they started walking down the long hallway. "So anyway," Gill continued, whispering, "this guy on that show was like crazy, right? His eyes were even freaky. Like cross-eyed, only the other way—both pointing out. But he dated these ladies so he could betray their trust and get into all their checking accounts and rob 'em of every cent they owned. Freaky. He even—"

"Can we *please* change the subject?" Lamar pleaded.

"What?"

"I don't think Lamar wants to hear stories about freaky dates," Alfonzo said.

"Sor-ry. I'm just trying to get my mind off my mom having that . . . kid."

Matt rolled his eyes. Well, at least it wasn't a *thing* anymore . . .

Gill continued, "You know what happened last night? They took one of my pictures off the wall and replaced it with a picture of the sonogram. *The sonogram!* A picture of the kid in my mom's stomach! You know what it looks like? A white blur surrounded by a black blur. I've been replaced by a *blur!*"

"Shhh!" Matt gritted his teeth. "I'm not sure this is the time, Gill."

"Well, what do you want to talk about, then?"

Matt took the opportunity. "Hey, Alfonzo, how's Iz?" he whispered.

Alfonzo's head dropped. "Are you going to ask me about her every day? Tell you what. If you want, I can pass her a duck-shaped note and she can check a box to let you know if she likes you."

"Really?"

"No!" everyone said at once.

"Quiet!" Matt retorted. "I hear something!"

The boys froze. Ahead they saw a set of double doors. They could hear muffled voices coming from the other side.

"The lunchroom?" Alfonzo asked.

Matt nodded. "Yeah, I think so. Or maybe the gymnasium."

The four boys tiptoed the rest of the way to the doors. Matt lightly pressed down on the latch of the door handle and it clicked. Ever so slowly he pulled on the handle to open the door.

The voices inside became clearer, one distinctly Oscar's voice, the other Matt recognized as the voice from the phone. Oscar's voice was uncharacteristically gruff, a tone Matt hadn't heard the man use before.

Matt spied a series of folded lunch tables just to the right of the door. With his head he motioned toward his friends and slipped into the room. One by one the boys slid in, unnoticed by Oscar and another man, and took refuge behind the lunch tables.

Matt leaned to his left and peeked through an opening between a table and a bench. The other boys found spy spots, too. Oscar was dressed completely in black, wearing the same jacket he'd worn yesterday in Lamar's kitchen. Even his shirt was black, accenting the golden jewelry that dangled from his neck and his wrists and sparkled from his knuckles. Though the room was only lit by some dirty skylights, Oscar sported dark sunglasses. He stared straight ahead at the other man, his arms folded neatly across his chest.

Oscar's friend, a younger black man, held a pamphlet of some kind in his hand, rolled up like a bat. His shirt was too big for his body, and his pants were baggy. His eyes were wide and his nostrils flared as he spoke.

"Give me a break!" Baggy Pants shouted emphatically. "I only—"

"Give you a break? Give you a break?!" Oscar didn't move a muscle but spoke loudly. "I've been giving you breaks, Sloan. *Too many* breaks."

Oscar stepped forward. The man he called Sloan stepped back.

"What? You gonna break my legs if I don't pay up? Is that the way ya do things?"

"I don't break legs," Oscar said matter-of-factly. A rush of relief brushed over Sloan's face. Oscar took another step forward. "I put them in cement."

"I thought he was a loan officer!" Gill whispered.

Alfonzo shook his head. "More like a loan *shark.*"

"What's that?"

"A guy who gives out loans and charges really high interest—and if you don't pay up ..."

"Don't hurt me, man!" Sloan shouted. "I got a wife! Kids!"

"And I gotta answer to *the man!*" Oscar shouted, his voice bouncing off the walls of the auditorium.

Suddenly Oscar reached into his jacket pocket and pulled out a handgun. The boys all jumped back and hit the wall with a slam.

Oscar and Sloan whirled around, surprised by the sudden sound. Oscar shoved his gun back in his jacket.

Matt looked at Lamar. Lamar looked at Gill. Gill looked at Alfonzo.

"Run!" Matt yelled.

"Who's there?" Oscar shouted.

Bam! Matt hit the door and rushed out. Lamar, Gill, and Alfonzo were right behind him, all of them crashing out of the room. They took off down the hall, trying to keep from slipping on the smooth surface as they raced back to the greenhouse.

Bam! Behind them they heard Oscar and Sloan hit the door, exiting the lunchroom. The men's footsteps echoed in the hall behind the boys.

"Whoozat?" Sloan shouted.

Crack! Matt and his friends ran into the greenhouse, shooting out the other side. They tore across the old school yard and rounded the side of the building. They heard the greenhouse door pop open behind them and more running steps.

"I told you he had a gun!" Matt shouted as the boys ran to the dumpster.

"You didn't tell me!" Alfonzo yelled.

They nearly toppled over each other as they grabbed their bikes, jumped on them, and took off. Fortunately, an incline appeared almost immediately and, pedaling their bikes as fast as they could down the hill, they left the school behind in a matter of seconds.

The boys kept glancing over their shoulders to see if they were being followed. About a mile later Matt angled to the right and slid into an alley behind a Happy Gas gas station, where he screeched to a halt. Lamar, Gill, and Alfonzo slammed on their brakes and slid into formation beside him.

They all stayed silent for a long moment as they caught their breath, their hearts beating like pistons in a car.

"You think he saw us?" Matt asked.

Lamar shook his head. "I don't think so. It was pretty dark in there—and we were *way* ahead of them. I don't think they followed us."

"I feel sick," Gill whimpered. "I think *I'm* gonna have a baby."

"What was that all about, anyway?" Alfonzo said.

"I don't think I want to know," Gill said.

"We have to call the police," Alfonzo said.

"On that show"—Gill was still gasping for breath—"*America's Most Dangerous*, they said you have to have evidence."

Matt nodded. "Gill's right. We don't have enough solid evidence. All we know is that he fooled all of us with his clean act—and he's clearly not who he presents himself to be. He even used contractions in there."

"So what do we do?" Lamar wondered aloud. "Do we try to find out more?"

Matt put his hand on Lamar's shoulder. "No—we just need to get you outta this."

"Me, nothin'," Lamar shot back. "We've gotta get this guy away from my *mom*."

Matt knew what to do. "Let's get the laptop."

4

Gill à la Carte

"Y ou sure this is going to work?" Lamar asked, biting a fingernail.

Matt, propped up behind his laptop, assured his friend. "How can it go wrong? Have we ever messed up before?"

"We got my dad fired," Gill said, sitting next to Matt.

"We blew up a house," added Alfonzo, who was across from Matt.

"We made Gill throw up on Hulk," Lamar pointed out.

Matt stared at his friends gathered around the circular booth in the restaurant. "Okay, but we got your dad a better job, Hulk's not mad at Gill, and . . . well . . . the house wasn't really our fault. Hulk's the one who opened the door."

Matt's eyes drifted to the entryway. Lamar's mom and Oscar would arrive at any moment. For he had typed in his laptop,

> Oscar Brown and Lorraine Whitmore walked
> into the high-class joint La Soupe à la
> Carte for a fine soup-and-salad lunch.
> And a shrimp appetizer. Because, let's
> face it, Oscar is loaded.

When Matt, Lamar, Gill, and Alfonzo had arrived, they had made sure they found the perfect place to sit: in a horseshoe booth, which was connected to another horseshoe booth—just right for Oscar and Lorraine. It was especially appropriate since between the two booths was white latticework with green ivy that blocked any view of the boys sitting right next door. It was the ideal place to type a story and change it as needed. Matt typed,

> Oscar Brown and Lorraine Whitmore sat in
> the booth next to where the QoolQuad
> were sitting.

Matt smiled. All too easy. Now they just had to wait.

"Ello," said a tall waiter in a white shirt, black bow tie, and black slacks. As he spoke, Matt surmised that his French accent was created just for the job. "Welcome to La Zoupe à la Carte. My name is

Jean-Luc and I am your waiter today. Our five zoups of ze day are La Zoupe à l'Oignon, La Zoupe au Pistou, La Bouillabaisse, L'Aïgo Boulido, and La Potage des Poireaux et Pommes de Terre."

The boys blinked.

"While you zink about zat, I can take your order for drinks."

He nodded to Gill.

"Uh, water."

Matt: "Water, please."

Lamar: "Water."

Alfonzo: "The same."

"Ah," the waiter said, "you've all made fine choices. Our premium bottled water comes straight from ze flowing springs of Zwitzerland."

He started to turn when Matt corrected him. "Uh, no, we just want regular water."

 The waiter bit his lip and looked at the four boys' faces. Lamar, Gill, and Alfonzo nodded agreement. The waiter's mouth made a popping sound and then he said, "Okay, exzellent choice. Four tap waters, flowing straight from ze aquifers of ze city zewers. May I interest you in an appetizer?"

The boys shook their heads.

"Of course not." The waiter spun on his heels and walked away.

"Maybe we should order something," Matt suggested.

"The soup is like fifteen dollars a bowl!" Lamar whispered as though it were a secret. "Anyone have that kind of cash on them?"

The others shook their heads.

"Okay, four zewer waters," Matt said, mimicking the waiter.

They laughed.

"Where's the bathroom?" Gill asked.

Matt rolled his eyes. "Mention water and Gill's gotta go."

"Do not! It's just . . . what if Sam shows up?"

"Sam's not gonna show up."

"How do you know? Aren't you afraid he might show up when you least expect it . . . again?"

"No. And if he does, I'll be ready."

"With what?"

"My wit."

"Oh, what a relief."

"They're here!" Alfonzo pointed toward the restaurant's entryway. The four boys' heads swung around. Oscar and Lamar's mom stood across the room, talking to a hostess. Oscar wore a blue suit this time, without any noticeable bulge in his jacket. Matt didn't notice any sunglasses or expensive gold jewelry on his person, either. He almost looked like a different man:

lighter, nicer, and without a care in the world. It was as if he had left his evil twin at home. Complementing him, Lorraine Whitmore wore a conservative purple dress with ruffles at the ends of her sleeves.

"Menus up!" Matt ordered. The four boys popped their large menus up in front of their faces. Matt put his up in front of his laptop and hunkered down behind it.

Matt felt prickles crawl down his neck as he heard Oscar and Lorraine sit behind him. Once they were seated, the boys set down their menus, since they were well hidden behind the latticework and ivy.

Oscar ordered raspberry tea for his date and himself . . . and a shrimp appetizer.

"So far, so good," Matt said quietly.

"Here's your tap water!"

The four boys jumped as Jean-Luc clanked four glasses down on the table. He pushed aside the cloth-covered cart he had used to roll them over and waited. When no one spoke up, he asked, "Have you decided what you want for lunch?"

"Where's the bathroom?" Gill asked.

Jean-Luc rolled his eyes and pointed to the back of the restaurant.

Gill started to get up but Matt grabbed his arm.

"Actually," Alfonzo whispered to the waiter, "I think the waters will be enough for now. But don't worry. We'll give you a twenty percent tip."

"Wonderful," Jean-Luc muttered. "I can't wait to zee what twenty percent of *nothing* will be."

"That waiter has a real attitude problem," Gill noted after the man left with his cart.

Matt turned to his friends. "So what's going to happen?"

"What do you mean?" Lamar asked, an anxious look on his face.

"I mean, what are we gonna make happen?"

"You don't know? You're the writer!"

"Do I look like I've had time to outline? Develop deep plot points? Examine the souls of my characters?"

"I thought you did that last night," Lamar said.

"I had chores."

"You've got to be kidding."

"So what's going to happen? Let's brainstorm."

"Yeah, and fast," Gill said as the waiter brought Oscar and Lorraine their shrimp cocktail on a cart. "I gotta go."

Matt thought for a long moment, trying to apply one of his best creativity starters. *What if . . . the restaurant caught on fire? What if . . . a tornado suddenly blew into town? What if . . .*

Lamar seemed to read his thoughts. "We can't be mean. I just want to turn my mom off to him."

Matt twisted his lip. "You want me to give him gas?"

"You can do that?"

Matt shrugged.

"No, that'll make *us* suffer, too. Something simpler."

"I got it," Matt said. Quickly he typed,

```
Right in the middle of a bite of shrimp,
Oscar sneezed a nasty sneeze.
```

Matt hit the key with the clock face on it, and at once the cursor changed to a golden clock that ticked forward like lightning. The four boys leaned over and peeked through the ivy.

"... took him to the market, he might enjoy the jazz," Oscar was saying.

"Maybe, maybe. He just needs time," Ms. Whitmore replied. "He's never faced it before. Lord knows it took me fourteen years."

Gill whispered, "Well?"

"Patience!" Matt whispered back.

Oscar picked up a shrimp, inspected it, and then stuffed it in his mouth. As he started to chew, his face began to contort.

The boys' eyes opened wide.

"Ah-*chooooooo!*"

Fwop! At once the shrimp shot out of his mouth. It sailed through the air toward Lamar's mom, who dodged it. It flew over her shoulder and smacked right into the arm of Jean-Luc.

Matt, Lamar, Gill, and Alfonzo jumped away from the screen and tried to keep from bursting with laughter.

"Zank you," Jean-Luc said flatly to Oscar.

"I apologize," Oscar said to him. "I do not know what came over me."

Jean-Luc headed toward the kitchen.

Lorraine looked shocked. "Use your napkin, child!" she finally said and then started laughing.

Matt looked at Gill. Gill looked at Alfonzo. Alfonzo looked at Lamar. Lamar looked back at Matt. "It didn't work," Lamar said. "She thinks he's adorable."

Matt shook his head. "I don't get it. I spill chocolate cake on Isabel and she gets furious. Oscar spits shrimp at Lamar's mom and she thinks it's cute."

"Yeah, but you ruined her dress," Alfonzo said.

Matt shrugged. "Okay, I'll raise the stakes." He typed,

> Right in the middle of a bite of shrimp
> covered in cocktail sauce, Oscar sneezed
> a nasty sneeze.

The boys pressed into the ivy-covered lattice-work.

"Anyway, I'm just saying he'll come around," Lamar's mom said to Oscar.

The man nodded, dipped a shrimp into a small bowl of red cocktail sauce, and sloshed it around. When it was thickly covered in the sauce, he shoved it into his mouth.

Suddenly his jaw froze.

The boys' eyes opened wide.

He reached for his napkin, but before he could get it to his mouth . . .

"Ah-*choooooo!*"

Fwop-pop-pop! Like a bullet, the shrimp flew out, this time toward the table. It bounced twice and ended up in Lamar's mother's lap. She jumped and let out a little scream.

Matt, Lamar, Gill, and Alfonzo jumped away from the screen.

Lamar's mom tried to smile this time, but it wasn't very convincing. She lifted her napkin off her lap and used it to remove the shrimp from her purple dress. The blotch of shrimp sauce didn't come off so easily, no matter how much she dipped her napkin into her water and dabbed at it.

Suddenly Matt didn't feel so good. He tried to remind himself that they were doing this to save Lamar's mom from heartache, but giving her trouble didn't seem to be the best route.

"I am *so* sorry, Lorraine," Oscar apologized.

"It's all right," she replied. "But I think we've had enough of the shrimp."

"Oh no!" Alfonzo nearly shouted aloud.

"What?" Matt, Lamar, and Gill asked at the same time, their heads swinging to him momentarily.

"Papa and Iz are here!"

"Isabel's here?" Matt asked.

Lamar pointed to the laptop. "Concentrate!"

Isabel and her father were on their way out when Isabel looked over and saw the boys. She was dressed in black jeans and a red blouse that accented her midnight black hair tumbling down her back like a waterfall. Isabel and her father waved to them and Alfonzo waved back. Isabel excused herself. Her father exited the restaurant and she headed over to the table.

"Alfonzo!" Lamar cried. "What are they doing here?"

"Today's their date!" Alfonzo exclaimed in a hush. "They always go to fancy places on their dates."

Gill hopped up. "If this is intermission, I'm going to the bathroom."

Matt grabbed his arm. "It can't wait? You always have to go in difficult situations! Remember the bank? Remember what happened?"

"I have no control over my bladder's whims!"

"Obviously," Matt retorted, letting go. "Just stay down, okay?"

Gill nodded and took off in a hunched position, passing Isabel. He smiled at her and continued on his way.

Just before she stepped up to the table, Matt slammed the laptop shut and covered it with his menu.

"Hey, Iz," Alfonzo said quietly.

"Hey, guys!" she said way too loudly. She didn't look at Matt.

"Shhh!" Alfonzo hushed his sister.

Isabel glanced at Matt, then looked at Lamar, then Alfonzo. "All right, what's going on?" she demanded, folding her arms across her chest.

Suddenly Ms. Whitmore stood up.

Alfonzo's eyes grew round and he jumped up and pushed Isabel into Gill's space, beside Matt. She yelped and Matt shoved Gill's menu in her face. "Read the menu!" he ordered.

"I've already eaten!" she shot back. Just then Lamar's mom walked by. But the woman was too busy studying the shrimp sauce stain on her dress to notice them.

Isabel grabbed the menu and flipped it over. "Oh, look!" she said, rather loudly again. "The dessert menu! I could have chocolate cake!" Then she turned to Matt. "Oh, never mind. I have some of that on my dress at home already."

Matt just stared at his menu. Lamar's mom disappeared into the bathroom and the boys set their menus down.

"What's going on?" Isabel's deep brown eyes caught Alfonzo's brown eyes. "Tell me or I'm telling Papa."

Without a moment's hesitation Alfonzo whispered, "You remember me telling you about the dangerous guy Lamar's mom is dating?"

Isabel nodded.

"Well, they're in that booth!"

Isabel's mouth dropped open. Her eyes grew wide and she leaned back, looking over. Then she leaned forward and whispered something in Spanish to Alfonzo. He whispered back. She said something else and he responded.

After a few more exchanges Lamar requested, "English, please—this is *my* mom, remember?"

Isabel held Alfonzo's stare for a few more moments and then leaned toward Lamar. "Your mom isn't going to drop him just because he's clumsy."

Matt turned to Isabel. "She isn't?"

Isabel turned to Matt and her eyes swallowed him up. "No," she said. "A girl's heart is stronger than that."

Matt felt his mouth turn upward. "I knew it was."

"But that doesn't mean clumsiness won't upset her," Isabel said. She turned back toward Lamar. "If you're going to get her out of this, she's got to see that she misjudged him. She needs to realize she made a serious mistake."

Lamar didn't say a word. Isabel stood up, her arm brushing Matt's. "I have to go. Papa has the car by now. Lemme know how it goes. Have fun."

Matt watched her leave, each step more graceful than the last. After she left the restaurant, he turned to Alfonzo. "You didn't tell her about the laptop, did you?"

"No," Alfonzo assured him. "I just told her we were hoping to trip him up—make him look clumsy."

"Good."

Gill came out of the bathroom and had walked halfway to the table when Lamar's mom came out of the women's bathroom. The menus went up immediately. Matt peeked over the top of his. Gill was looking around to see what the alarm was. When he spotted Lamar's mom, he dived down, taking refuge under one of the cloth-covered carts.

Ms. Whitmore stepped past him, then past the boys' table, to finally turn and sit at her own. Oscar immediately broke into a series of apologies, all of which she accepted.

"What are we going to do?" Lamar asked as they dropped their menus again.

Matt looked at his laptop and threw his hands up in the air.

Suddenly Jean-Luc appeared, placed his hands on the cart Gill was under, and rolled it across the room. The three boys' eyes grew wide as he wheeled it right in front of Oscar and Lorraine's table.

"Oh no," Lamar said.

"Oh no," Alfonzo echoed.

"Just stay under there!" Matt whispered as loudly as he could.

Jean-Luc removed the shrimp and napkins from Oscar and Lorraine's table and set them on the cart. Suddenly, as if an earthquake were upon them, the cart began to shake and a cackling sound came from underneath.

"Ha ha!" Gill's laugh filled the restaurant, the cart rumbling.

Jean-Luc flipped the cloth up and jumped back when he saw Gill underneath, laughing and pointing to the beeper on his side. "Make it stop! Ha ha! Make it stop!"

Ms. Whitmore hopped up. "Gill Gillespie?"

Matt, Lamar, and Alfonzo jumped up.

Then she turned and saw the boys. "Lamar? Boys! What are you doing here?"

Lamar glared at Oscar. "Trying to save you from a serious mistake!" he blurted to his mother.

"Try to get to know me," Oscar pleaded, standing up.

Gill continued to cackle until Jean-Luc yanked the beeper off his waist, calming him down.

"Lamar Taylor Whitmore, you go home this minute," his mother ordered. "We'll discuss this later."

In a huff, Lamar pushed Alfonzo out of the booth and exited the restaurant. Alfonzo looked at Matt and Matt grabbed his laptop. They gave an awkward wave to Lamar's mom and Oscar and hurried toward the door. Matt turned back in time to see Gill, still underneath the cart, retrieve his beeper, pull down the sheet, and wheel himself out.

Feeling as dreary as the cool evening weather, Matt waddled down his driveway, tin garbage can in front of him, ready to drop the junk at the curb and call it a day. A very *bad* day.

Matt thunked the can at the corner—and that's when he saw her, standing across the street at her mailbox. Isabel Zarza.

Matt felt his breath escape slowly as he stood up straight and wished there were something nearby to lean on, to help him look casual and cool. Isabel smiled softly and waved weakly, her fingers tumbling one after another. Matt waved back in similar fashion.

"So are you going to come over and talk to me, or are you going to make me yell across the street?" she shouted with a smile.

Matt returned a smirk. "I, uh, was just on my way over." He started across the street, the butterflies in his stomach fluttering faster with each step. He rubbed the goose bumps off his cold, exposed arms and stopped in front of her.

Isabel brushed a lock of her long, straight black hair out of her eyes. She wore blue jeans and a pink T-shirt advertising a Latino band Matt had never heard of.

"So . . . ," Matt began, not sure what else to say. He looked at the ground.

"I heard about what happened," Isabel said.

"Yeah," Matt said. "Gill's mom just had another false alarm. Gill is so upset. I think it's just big brother jitters, but—"

Isabel giggled. "No, I mean I heard what happened with Lamar."

Matt cracked a smile. "Oh, right. Yeah, he's sentenced to help out at church for the next month, I think. Pastor Ruhlen will be thrilled."

"You really haven't had a lot of success at eating out lately, have you?"

Matt looked up. "Not funny."

"I never said I was a comedian. I'm a realist."

"Same difference."

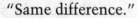 For a long moment both were silent, staring at the ground. Then, at the same second, they both looked up. "I'm sorry," they said at the same time.

Isabel giggled again.

Matt chuckled. "Thanks," he said. "So you, uh, really forgive me for being clumsy?"

Isabel smiled. "If you'll forgive me for getting so angry."

"I deserved it."

"I know." But her eyes twinkled.

Matt laughed. "Okay, yeah, I did deserve it. I'm really sorry about the chocolate cake."

Isabel looked down the street and let out a long breath. "It wasn't the chocolate cake. There's . . . more to it." She breathed deeply. Her voice cracked. "I think you just struck a cord from—"

"I know," Matt said, nodding. "From your mom leaving and all. No sweat. I understand."

"You understand?"

"Oh yeah. I know—"

"You *don't* know. There's a *whole lot* more to me than what you know."

"Don't get upset," Matt pleaded.

"Well, don't turn all Dr. Phil on me, then."

"Why are you getting so mad?"

"Mad? You haven't seen *mad!*" Isabel turned on her heel and headed back to her house.

For a moment Matt just stood there, stunned. The shock was broken when his dad pulled into the driveway in his Ford F-150. Just as Isabel entered her house and slammed the door, Matt's dad, a construction manager, stepped out of his pickup. Matt crossed the street, kicking the curb on his way. As Matt passed him, his dad said, "Hey, Ace, how come every time I see that girl, she's walking *away* from you?"

"Apparently," Matt responded, "it's because *I don't know.*"

Matt's dad nodded. "Girls."

5

Intervention

Dudes!" Pastor Ruhlen shouted. "The only thing good about you gettin' in trouble is that I get to see ya more!"

Lamar stuffed a tuft of blue tissue into an octagon of chicken wire. "Yeah, but helping you build your float isn't helping me forget about my problems."

"Point taken!" Pastor Ruhlen said with a wink. He bobbed his head, his sky blue Chia Pet hair bouncing forward. The surfer-turned-youth-pastor was always a sight to behold, with ever changing hair.

"Though, bro," Pastor Ruhlen added, "this is the church's float, not mine. I'm just the one knock-knockin' it together."

Matt looked at the boxes of blue tissue paper lying on the ground like a toppled tower of bricks. Maybe a hundred of them. "So what's the float gonna be?" he asked.

"That's a surprise!" Ruhlen replied. "Hafta wait to see."

"Hey, losers!"

Everyone's heads snapped to the sidewalk leading up to Pastor Ruhlen's apartment complex.

"What're you doing here, Hulk?" Pastor Ruhlen asked when Hulk Hooligan joined the group.

"I jus' wanted ta help my fellow churchgoers," he replied, sounding like Rocky.

Pastor Ruhlen pulled his wire-rim sunglasses down his nose, his green eyes piercing Hulk.

Hulk buckled. "'K, I got caught givin' swirlies ta some nerds in school again. Dad said I had ta come."

Lamar held out his hand. "Nice to be serving penance with you."

Hulk ignored the offered hand. "Not dat I do whatever my dad says," he added. He grabbed the nearest tissue box and pulled out a blue tissue. He blew his nose in it and then stuffed it into the chicken wire.

"Dudes!" Pastor Ruhlen shouted, making everybody jump. "Why don't you join me on this float, man? We can rock the parade!"

Lamar stuffed another blue tissue into the wire.

"Dudes! It'll be a rockin' blast-o-rama! I'm gonna sing a short duet with Suzie Brantley, and then I'm blastin' music and throwin' out candy!"

"Doesn't sound so bad," Matt admitted.

"Yeah! But to win most exciting float, I need more! I want background dancers who can do the Macarena!"

"*That* sounds bad," Matt said.

Pastor Ruhlen thumped the side of his head with his finger. "I got the vision up here," he said. "Okay, maybe not the Macarena, but some sort of choreographed dance. Hey, if ya wanna do it, we can practice in the youth hall at church. Dudes, the stage is still set up from the winter play. Just pop in a CD, turn on the spotlight, and you'll be jammin', sweatin' to the oldies, like TobyMac on the track!"

Hulk protested. "No way I'm dancin' on dis float. Last time I was in da spotlight, I got puked on." He glared at Gill, who shrunk back.

"It could make you famous again," Matt said, toying with Hulk. "I'm sure a lot of people would get a good laugh out of your dancing."

Hulk's head swung in Matt's direction. His eyes narrowed to slivers. "Ya don't even know if I can dance. Think ya know all about me, do ya, Calhan? Pegged me as a dumb bully, have ya?"

Matt shook his head. "This coming from the guy who pegged us all as losers the second he laid eyes on us."

"Yeah," Hulk admitted, "but *I* was right."

Pastor Ruhlen nodded. "Guys, we should give Hulk a chance to prove himself. Hulk, you can dance if you want."

"Not in a gazillion years."

"You guys!" Lamar yelled, jolting everyone. "Forget the parade! We have more important things to deal with!"

The group fell quiet for a long moment until Lamar started stuffing tissue again.

Pastor Ruhlen flashed a wide smile. "Yeah, let those emotions out, dude. Let it flow. Get rid o' that anger." Then he turned to Matt. "What's he talkin' 'bout, Willis?" Pastor Ruhlen often called people by a made up name.

Matt knew Lamar wouldn't mind if he explained. "He's not too thrilled about Oscar."

"You talking about the cat his mom's datin'? The dude who paid for all the snot rags for this float?"

Alfonzo nodded. "That's who he's talking about."

"Yeah," Matt said. "Hey, what do you know about him?"

The youth pastor propped a foot up on the back of the float. "He seemed like a pretty decent hombre to me. I don't know him too well, I guess."

"He's a sheep in wolves' clothing," Lamar responded frankly.

"Can you keep a secret?" Matt asked the youth pastor.

He nodded.

"We can't say how," Matt said, "but we know he's snowing everyone."

"Well," Pastor Ruhlen said, "you know, people ain't always what you expect. Jesus said in Luke 6:37, 'Do not judge, and you will not be judged.' Dude, we have to leave the judging to the Big Guy upstairs."

"But people judge others all the time," Matt said.

"Right-e-o," Pastor Ruhlen replied. "But you're a writer, Matt. You know you have to know what's inside a book before judging it. You can't get careless with your thoughts and judge a book by its cover."

Matt shifted his feet. "Yeah, but how do you know what's inside?"

"Oh yeah!" Pastor Ruhlen exclaimed. "Jesus said you can recognize people by the fruit they bear, man—that's Matthew, chapter seven. Look at a guy's actions. Listen to his words. See how he lives his life."

Lamar stopped stuffing. "That's just it, Pastor Ruhlen," he said. "We've seen the truth—we've seen his actions . . . even though he doesn't know it." He grimaced. "I just don't know how we can get him to fess up to my mom."

Pastor Ruhlen stuffed another blue tissue into the wire. "Well, have you guys tried talking to him?"

Pedaling their bikes at full speed, the boys headed straight to Lamar's house.

"You sure this is what Pastor Ruhlen meant?" Alfonzo asked.

"Sure," Matt assured his friend. "It's called an intervention. I've seen them in the movies. We need to confront him—lay everything out on the table."

As the boys rounded the corner onto Oleander Street, they saw Oscar standing behind his car in Lamar's driveway. When he spotted the boys, he quickly closed the trunk and pocketed the keys.

The boys came to a screeching halt in front of Oscar, the back tires of their bikes streaking the ground with black marks.

"Whoa!" Oscar exclaimed.

The boys straddled their bikes and faced Oscar.

"Hi, boys," Oscar said cautiously.

The boys didn't say a word.

"Hey, about yesterday at the restaurant," Oscar said, his eyes on Lamar. "Do you really feel like I am a mistake for your mother?"

"I do," Lamar said firmly, clutching the handle-bars of his bike, as if to keep his hands from shaking.

Oscar bit his lip. "I see."

"I thought you said you were a loan officer," Lamar said in a challenging tone.

 Oscar's eyes shifted to the house and back to the boys. "I am." Then he smiled. "Boys, I do not know what this is about, but—"

"We know your secret," Matt stated plainly.

Oscar's lips tightened. "What?"

"Your secret," Matt repeated. "We know all about it."

Oscar was quiet for a long moment as his mouth turned down. Then he asked, "What secret?"

"Your little act here," Lamar said boldly.

Oscar let out a short breath. "How did you find out?"

"We followed you," Alfonzo said.

Oscar nodded slowly. "That was you ... back at the school?"

"Yes," Lamar said. "So it's time you fessed up to my mom."

Oscar narrowed his eyes. "Why should I? I don't want her to know."

"I'm sure you don't. But if you don't tell her, I will."

"Lamar, you cannot force me to do this." Then Oscar's face changed and a shadow fell over it. "Do not tell her."

"Or what? You'll start using contractions?"

Coolly Oscar slipped his hand into his jacket. Matt froze. He was going for the gun.

Bam!

Everyone jumped. Oscar's hand flew out of his jacket and the boys nearly fell over like dominoes. Ms. Whitmore stood in the doorway of her house, the screen door slamming open against the siding.

"Lamar Taylor Whitmore!" Her voice was loud and sharp. "What's going on?"

"Let Oscar tell you," Lamar said firmly.

"My secret stays a secret," Oscar whispered to Lamar. "You understand?"

Lamar stared at the bulge in Oscar's jacket. He reluctantly nodded. Oscar smiled at Lorraine and then popped the driver's door to his black Cadillac. "Everything is fine," he said, slipping in. He gave the QoolQuad one last stare and then closed the door. A moment later he backed down the driveway. Another moment and his car disappeared around the corner.

"What on earth is going on, Lamar?" Ms. Whitmore demanded again.

"I don't like him," Lamar muttered.

"What?"

"I don't like him," Lamar repeated, his voice shifting up a notch.

"Lamar, I will not have you drive him off. You need to give him a chance."

"He's not a good man, Ma."

"Boy, do not judge someone you don't know."

"I'm not, Ma. I know what you need—and it's not someone like that."

"No one's gonna replace your daddy," Ms. Whitmore said, her left hand on her hip.

"It's not that!" Lamar exclaimed. "Why does everyone think it's about that? You have to trust me, Ma. You're misjudging that guy!"

"That *guy's* name is Oscar," Ms. Whitmore said plainly, raising her voice. "And outside of you, boy, he's the best thing that's happened to me in the last fourteen years. You will *not* run him off because you're judging him without knowing him!"

"Me? *You* don't know him, Ma!" Lamar's face tightened with anger. "You don't know him because you don't want to know him! You want to believe the best because you *want* to replace Dad! Well, I don't! Not with someone who's just going to break your heart!"

Lamar turned his bike and took off down the street.

"Lamar! Lamar Whitmore! Come back here!"

Lamar didn't look back. He just kept pedaling as fast as he could.

Ms. Whitmore's hand slipped to her mouth as tears formed in her eyes.

"We'll find him," Matt promised, nodding to Gill and Alfonzo. They all swung around and rode their bikes out of the driveway.

The "sewer station," as Matt and Lamar called it, was a small brick building a block and a half away from their houses. It had one solid door, no windows, and if you listened closely, you could hear water rushing through the pipes inside. With his bike propped up beside him, Matt sat in the gravel at the rear of the building, waiting. It didn't take long for Lamar to show.

His best friend came coasting into the secluded hiding place, slid to a stop, and looked at Matt.

"How'd you know I'd come here?" he asked.

Matt grinned. He tilted the screen of his laptop so Lamar could read it.

At precisely 5:45 Lamar biked to the sewer station.

Lamar sighed. "I hate it when you use that thing on me."

Matt shrugged. He shut the laptop and slid it into his backpack. Lamar propped his bike up beside Matt's. He crashed on the gravel beside Matt and stared forward into the chain-link fence rooted in wayward weeds and rubble.

"You'd have come here anyway," Matt said.

Lamar nodded. "Probably right."

A good ten minutes passed without either of them saying a word. They just stared ahead and down at the gravel.

"Where are the guys?" Lamar finally asked.

"Alfonzo had to go to dinner. Gill went to see if there was any news on his little monster."

Lamar smirked. He shuffled through the gravel for a rock. He found one with sharp corners and pitched it at the fence. It hit a chain-link and bounced back. "You remember the first time we came here?"

"Like yesterday," Matt said.

"Second grade, right?"

"Yes. Hulk's first day of school with us. He came in and terrorized all the guys. Kept pushing us into the urinals."

Lamar chuckled. "Yeah, until you stepped in."

"Yeah, I waited until he got behind me and then stomped on his foot."

"I'll never forget it. He screamed like a girl."

"And then he came after me. I ran all the way here—six blocks—and lost him somewhere along the way."

"Man, Miss Fritel was freaked. All she knew was that you took off out of school like your pants were on fire and that no one could find you."

"*You* found me."

"And you're lucky. You were gonna stay here all night."

"I didn't want a knuckle sandwich," Matt admitted.

"You didn't get one."

"I know. Fortunately for me, Tony Nedbit hit Hulk in dodge ball the next day and Hulk forgot all about me."

"Short attention span."

"Still, I'm glad we found this place."

Lamar nodded. "Me too. No telling how many times we came here and dreamed about being football stars."

"So much for that," Matt said.

"And how many times have we sworn we'd never get married, because—"

"Girls stink," both of them said in unison.

They laughed. Then Matt added, "Now I actually think some of them smell good."

Lamar threw another rock. "Things change. Ma always says things get harder the older you get."

"What's up with that?"

"I don't know. I guess we're growing older. How does Pastor Ruhlen say it?"

"Smarter, stronger, deeper, and cooler."

"Yeah," Lamar said. "Luke 2:52: 'And Jesus grew in wisdom and stature, and in favor with God and men.' We're growing smarter, stronger, deeper, and cooler, just like him."

"You're a walking Bible. You think Jesus faced junk like we do?"

"Worse—but he didn't give in to the fear. And that made all the difference." Lamar paused, then said, "So what are we gonna do?"

Matt leaned his head back on the brick wall, feeling his hair stick to the brick texture. "I don't know. He's dangerous, but we have no proof. It's his word against ours."

"And he's slick."

"Yep. Every scenario I play in my mind ends up with us wearing cement on our feet at the bottom of Lake Windham."

"If my mom marries this guy, I'm going to have to enter the witness protection program."

Matt smiled. "We won't let it get that far."

"You scared?" Lamar asked.

"Well, when something affects you, it affects me." After a pause Matt added, "But you know, for what it's worth, I think she's telling the truth when she says she's not trying to replace your dad."

"I know. It's just . . . I always thought when she dated, it'd be some great guy. You know, a guy on fire for God. Someone who lives the Bible. She deserves that. Instead she's lured to Grumpy."

"Dopey."

"Sneezy. And that's not right. It's not fair. And the more I warn her about him, the more dead-set she is about staying with him."

Matt nodded.

"So was Ma mad?"

"I counted two bulging veins—one in her neck, the other on her forehead."

Lamar nodded. "Yeah, I'd better get home."

Later that night Matt sat at his laptop, fingers on the keyboard, wondering what to do. He was in the middle of typing out his thoughts, outlining what-ifs, when his Instant Messaging program beeped.

Bing!

* Lamar is online. *

> Lamar: hey matt come up with any ideas?

Matt let out a long breath.

> MattC: Nope. Fresh out. You?
>
> Lamar: nope
>
> MattC: You're still alive?
>
> Lamar: yeah but mas really hung on this
> guy. she was crying and everything
>
> MattC: :(

There was a long pause and Matt went back to brainstorming. *What if... What if... What if...* About ten minutes later the program beeped again. *Bing!*

> * ALF is online. *

Matt chuckled. He typed,

> MattC: You gonna leave that as your user-
> name? You sound like a cat-munching alien.

> Lamar: ROTFL

Another long pause, followed by:

> ALF: Hi Lamar, it's Isabel.

Matt's eyes grew wide. "Guess you never know who you're really talking to," he whispered.

> Lamar: hey isabel. what's up?
>
> ALF: Not much. Alfonzo said you mighht be dannig on the church float
>
> ALF: * dancing

Matt typed,

> MattC: Not if I can help it

Isabel ignored him.

> ALF: If you want, I can teach you some doncing moves so you won't look so sily. I can good at dancing.

Matt's eyebrows shot up.

> MattC: You can dance?

> ALF: I told you there was more to me
> than you know
>
> ALF: Alfonzo wants to know if you
> thaught of anything to save your mom
> from this guy??
>
> Lamar: well we have a few tricks up our
> sleeves

Matt looked at his laptop. "We sure do."

> ALF: Well I can see wy he didn't come
> clean. It makes sene. No one wants to
> have their secrets exposed for the world
> to see.
>
> ALF: I mean we all have struggles.
> Things that are deeper than just out
> side appearances

Matt blinked. He reread what Isabel had written.

MattC: Lamar! That's it!

Lamar: what?

MattC: What Isabel said!

Lamar: about us all having struggles?

MattC: No! Before that!

Then he added,

MattC: Isabel, can you really teach us to dance?

6

In the Spotlight

So what changed your minds?" Pastor Ruhlen asked Matt, Lamar, Gill, Alfonzo, and Isabel as he flicked on the switch to the youth hall. As the fluorescent lights buzzed to life, the QoolQuad took in the youth stage, which was decorated with snowflakes, holly, and other Christmas icons. Bales of hay and wreaths peppered the stage and walls.

What changed their minds? *Oscar*, Matt thought. *And a brilliant plan.* Matt was glad he'd thought of it. Well, Isabel had sparked the idea, but . . .

The plan was simple: They had to expose the horrible truth about Oscar for Lamar's mother to see. But they had to do it publicly so Oscar couldn't retaliate. His hand had shot to his coat a little fast when they confronted him the other day. He was obviously unpredictable, so they needed to keep themselves—and Lamar's mother—safe.

They had pondered what would be the perfect setting. And, thanks to Isabel, Matt had conceived a radiant idea. Half the city of Enisburg would attend the upcoming annual parade. So Matt quickly convinced the guys that all they had to do was win first place in the parade with Pastor Ruhlen's float. When the victory announcement was made, Matt would make sure Oscar was called up on stage, since he had paid for the float . . . and then all masks would be removed for the world to see.

Lamar didn't answer Pastor Ruhlen's question. "Hey, for now I'm just glad to get my mind off everything."

Pastor Ruhlen clucked his tongue a few times. "Still havin' troubles getting settled in with ol' Oscar?"

Lamar nodded.

"It'll be fixed soon," Matt said. "But right now we need to get our dancing down."

Pastor Ruhlen's face lit up. "Right-e-o! It is so sa-weet that you dudes are gonna dancer-oo on the float with me! We're destined for first place for sure!"

"Well, we'll certainly try to do our best."

Pastor Ruhlen pointed the group to the stage and then retreated to the sound booth. He slipped a CD into the sound system, cued it up, and grabbed a remote control. Then he ran up to the stage, where the boys and Isabel now sat.

"Okay. The tune is a pop/rock mix I created on my keyboard. But before it starts, Suzie Brantley is singin' a slow duet with me. It's that worship song 'Search Me.'"

"Oh, I like that song," Isabel said.

Pastor Ruhlen winked. "Yeah, good stuff, Maynard."

Isabel squinted. "And it goes from the worship song into a pop/rock mix?"

Pastor Ruhlen smiled and his eyebrows hopped up. "Yeah."

"Hmm. That'll be interesting."

Pastor Ruhlen lifted the remote and pressed a button. A few seconds later the song flowed from the speakers. It was a peaceful, hollow sound with synthesized wind instruments and rolling percussion. Isabel closed her eyes, listening to the worship tune. Matt watched her take in the music. She seemed to settle into the worship tune easily. Oddly enough, when she and her brother first moved to Enisburg just a few months ago, neither had ever attended a church like Matt's. Now occasionally they came to youth group. Isabel always sat on the other side of the room with some girls from her school, so Matt hadn't seen her like this. But he could see now that her heart was really softened to God. He smiled. Now if he could just get her to talk to *him*. She hadn't said too much to him on the way over, though she seemed to have cooled off from his latest blunder.

Matt wondered how much better friends they might become if he could just keep his mouth shut.

A minute later the song kicked into high gear with a not-so-easy transition, picking up with a funky pop/rock beat.

Pastor Ruhlen handed Isabel the remote. "Go for it," he said.

After listening for a few more seconds, she hit the stop button. She backed the song up, started it again, and then stood. "Okay," she said. "Here's what would be cool. Let's start with your backs to Pastor Ruhlen and—what's her name?"

"Suzie," Pastor Ruhlen answered.

"Okay, start off with your backs to Pastor Ruhlen and Suzie, heads down." Isabel turned around and put her head down. "Like this. Then wait until the fast part starts up . . . here." Right when the pop/rock segment started pumping, she spun around, her black ponytail swishing behind her head. "Then start moving back and forth like this, to the beat. Let's go right hand cross, left hand cross, clap, clap, stomp, stomp, spin, repeat. Like this." She performed the dance segment all the way through a few times, spinning around and repeating. "See?" she said as she moved. "Easy. You can do this in your sleep."

Matt looked at Lamar. Lamar looked at Gill. Gill looked at Alfonzo. Alfonzo looked at Isabel.

"Anything my sister can do, I can do better," Alfonzo assured his friends.

The boys stood and Isabel skipped the CD back to the beginning of the song. She turned around and the four boys followed suit, standing behind her like shadows in four different spots.

When the fast part came, they all spun around. Matt crossed his hands, Lamar stomped his feet, Gill spun around, and Alfonzo did all three. Pastor Ruhlen twisted his lip.

Isabel giggled, her voice sounding like newly spun honey. "Wait! Stop! Stop!" she cried. She restarted the segment. "Like this. One, two, three, four. One, two, three, four." She danced to the beat as she had instructed. "Okay, join in."

This time Matt spun, Lamar crossed his hands, Gill stomped, and Alfonzo still did all three.

Isabel giggled again and put her hand on her forehead. "Can't you guys hear the beat?"

"You mean the drums?" Matt wondered.

Pastor Ruhlen's forehead wrinkled.

Isabel re-cued the song. "Okay, from the top."

The four boys tried time and again to follow Isabel. A half hour later she stopped the CD. "Okay!" she exclaimed. Then she muttered something under her breath in Spanish.

Alfonzo chuckled.

She looked up. "Is there room on the team for me too?" she asked Pastor Ruhlen.

The guys all looked a little surprised.

Isabel responded with a look of shock. "What? No girls allowed?"

"Hey!" Pastor Ruhlen shouted. "The more, the merrier! Maybe we could put you out front."

Matt, Lamar, Gill, and Alfonzo all nodded. "We need all the help we can get," Lamar admitted.

Isabel returned a smile. "Great. I'll take the center spot and you can all follow me."

The QoolQuad nodded agreement.

Pastor Ruhlen looked at his watch. "Hey, I gotta make a telly call, dudes. Be right back. Don't lose your rhythm while I'm gone!"

"Shouldn't be tough," Gill yelled after him. "We haven't found it yet!"

"Let's all take a break," Isabel suggested. "I need a drink. You all want one?"

Matt said, "Pepsi."

Lamar said, "Dew."

Gill said, "Dr. P."

Alfonzo said, "Orange."

Isabel smiled. "I'm getting water. Water for everyone!" And she exited the room.

The youth hall quiet, the four boys sat.

"We're hopeless, aren't we?" Alfonzo said.

"You guys are," Gill said, "but I was born for the spotlight."

"You and Hulk," Matt teased.

"Guys, this *has* to work," Lamar said. "It's the only way to save my mom."

"We'll get it," Matt said encouragingly.

"Yeah, but we have to be *good*," Lamar said.

Click! At once the lights went off. The room fell black, save dim columns of light sneaking through the rectangular windows on the side doors.

"Iz!" Alfonzo shouted. "Cut it out!"

Boom! With the power of the sun, a spotlight beamed in the boys' faces, making them jump up in surprise. Matt threw his right hand in front of his eyes. He squinted through his fingers, trying to see who was playing with them.

"Iz! That's bright!" Alfonzo shouted to his sister again.

"*Hello, Matt.*"

Matt's heart skipped a beat when he heard the familiar, eerie metallic voice.

"W-who is that?" Lamar asked.

The light from the doors played on the now familiar pair of thin cowboy boots.

"Guys, meet Sam," Matt responded. "Sam, the guys."

"I told you he'd show up!" Gill exclaimed, slapping Matt on the arm. "Is he gonna kill us?" he whimpered.

Matt shook his head. "Not yet."

"Your friends know, don't they, Matt?" Sam was speaking through some sort of electronic device, disguising his voice.

Matt nodded. No use in hiding the truth. "I thought you knew they knew."

"Matt, this must stay a secret. You can't trust anyone."

Matt stepped forward and pulled his hand down. "We've been over this," he challenged. "But I don't agree. I have friends I can trust. People are better than you think."

"Are they?"

"What do you want?" Matt demanded. He'd been scared out of his wits enough lately. "I'm being secretive with the laptop, just like you asked. No one's going to be able to trace it back to me."

"Don't underestimate them, Matt."

"Who?"

Sam didn't answer the question. *"Don't get careless with the laptop, Matt."*

"Look, we're only using it to expose scum," Matt continued.

"And make dreams come true," Lamar added weakly.

"Yeah," Matt agreed. "And help people like Gill's pregnant mom."

"Shhh!" Gill hushed Matt.

"Just be sure you know what you're doing," Sam warned. *"Remember, some things aren't what they seem."*

"Like you?" Matt asked, stepping forward again.

"There's a lot you don't know," Sam told him. *"A lot more you're about to know. All of you. I'll call on you when it's time."*

"Um, just for the record," Gill piped up, "you don't have to call on me."

Boom! The light popped off and the boys heard footsteps.

Click! The fluorescent ceiling lights buzzed on again and the guys screamed. A door at the back of the room slowly closed. Entering the side door, Isabel dropped her handful of bottled waters when she saw the boys' ashen faces.

"D-did I miss something?"

Can't Do Just a Du

Matt wasn't sure what to do with Lamar. For the past half hour he had paced back and forth in front of Matt like a crazed sentry.

"You're going to weaken the pavement," Matt warned him.

He just kept pacing.

For the past week leading up to the parade, nothing had changed. Isabel and the boys practiced their choreography. Endlessly. Pastor Ruhlen and Suzie Brantley practiced their worship song. Lamar was over at Matt's more than usual, and when he went home, he said he usually just went to his room. He told Matt it was like torture, watching his mother go out on dates with Oscar, knowing what he was really like . . . remembering what they had seen. Matt kept encouraging his friend to be patient, stick it out, and soon they would put the laptop to work.

Now it was Saturday morning—parade morning— and the crisp air was sure to promise a hearty turnout. On their way downtown, Matt had gazed up at the tallest buildings—Mochrie Financial, the Enisburg Hospital, Security Bank headquarters, and a Hilton hotel. He and his friends were about to ride the float past each of them, and Matt wondered what the view would be like from one of the top floors.

Stopped on Sydney Avenue, waiting for the parade to start, Matt sat on the curb, his computer in his lap. Like the other boys and Isabel, he wore a white dress shirt and black slacks. They looked like such a well-dressed quintet.

"What're you writing?" Lamar puffed warm air into his cupped hands.

Matt tilted his laptop's screen so Lamar could see.

```
Without a doubt, the QoolQuad put on the
most entertaining performance possible
so the Enisburg Community Church float
has a great chance at winning the float
contest at this year's annual parade.
```

"Isn't that a run-on sentence?"

Matt frowned and looked at the screen. But run-on sentences were the least of his concerns.

"Where is Pastor Ruhlen, anyway?" Matt asked as he hit the clock key. The cursor changed to the golden clock that swiftly ticked forward, somehow ensuring the future.

Lamar shrugged. "I don't know."

"Well," Matt said, closing his laptop, "we'll put forth our best effort, but this should help give us an edge. We don't need any misunderstandings."

"No, we certainly don't," Lamar agreed. "This is our one chance. Nothing is more important than getting it right. You know what happened last night?"

"Your mom and Oscar went out on another date?"

"No—just the opposite. It was Friday night and Oscar had 'business.' Can you imagine that? A 'loan officer' working on Friday night. I told my mom that was fishy, but she wouldn't hear of it. Then this morning, before he drove us here, he reaches into his pocket for his keys and guess what falls out."

"A rubber band, a nickel, and a half-eaten Snickers bar."

"Three one-hundred-dollar bills."

Matt's eyebrows shot up. "Whoa. What'd your mom say?"

"She didn't see. Oscar just looks at me and puts his finger over his lips. 'Shhh.'"

Matt's eyes narrowed. "He's goin' down."

"Yes, sir."

Matt glanced down the sidewalk and watched Isabel going over the dance steps with Gill and Alfonzo one last time. The boys were doing most of it on their own. Isabel had turned out to be a great teacher. He hadn't even known she could dance. It's not that Matt didn't think she *could*, it's just that he never expected it.

Lamar let out a long breath. "Still, I wish it didn't have to be like this. Why couldn't he just come clean?"

"We gave him more than enough chances," Matt assured his friend.

"I guess. It's just gonna break my mom's heart."

"Better now than later."

Lamar agreed.

"Hey, dudes!"

Matt and Lamar turned to see Pastor Ruhlen bounding up the sidewalk. His outfit was fiery red from neck to toe, matching his red hair. Hulk Hooligan, Hulk's dad, and Hulk's younger brother Nate followed behind him. Matt shoved his laptop into his backpack.

Pastor Ruhlen put out his hand and when Matt stood up and shook it, he pulled Matt's hand in, knocked it, lifted it, and swirled it around. Some kind of secret handshake of the eighties, Matt guessed. He forgot it as quickly as he could.

Nate ran over and gave Matt a hug. Despite being Hulk's brother, he was the sweetest little kid Matt knew.

"Hey, dudes, whadda ya think of our rippin' float?" Pastor Ruhlen pointed down the way.

Matt and Lamar took a few steps back. Matt squinted. "Where? We've been looking for it."

"Right behind the Wiz Plumbing float!" Pastor Ruhlen exclaimed.

Matt's mouth dropped. "You . . . you mean the float with the gigantic surf wave on top?"

"Fer sure!" Pastor Ruhlen nodded. "What did you think all those blue tissues were for? That's the biggest wave to ever crash down the Enisburg streets!"

Lamar frowned. "So surfing . . . going to church . . . Am I missing the connection?"

"Fun in the Son, dude! Get it? S–O–N!"

Matt winced. "Very . . . punny."

"Yeah, anyway, so Mr. Hooligan, Hulk, and Nate are gonna drive for us. We just hooked it up to his pickup. It'll be fun, won't it, Hulk?"

Hulk grunted.

"Yeah. That was a yes," Pastor Ruhlen interpreted. "I got a stage set up around the wave, with mikes, speakers, and plenty o' candy. You can put your pack in the front with Hulk."

Matt and Lamar caught eyes.

"Is there a sound booth on the float?" Matt asked.

"It's more of a box," Pastor Ruhlen said. "But yeah, it's up near the cab."

Matt nodded. "Okay, I can just put my backpack there." He looked at Hulk. "No use making you guys scrunch up to fit my junk in with you."

Hulk belched.

Pastor Ruhlen looked at his watch. "Where is Suzie?" He motioned to the pay phone across the street. "I'll be right back."

"Should we go down to the float?" Matt asked Mr. Hooligan.

He nodded and they turned, then—

Pop! Pop! Pop!

Everyone's eyes bugged when Lamar's mom stopped them in their tracks, snapping pictures like a photojournalist. Oscar was right beside her.

"Aw, Ma!" Lamar cried, shaking his head. "Warn us next time."

Lamar's mom and Oscar were both dressed for warmth. She wore a gray coat, he had on a woolen black jacket. She checked her son over from head to toe, then started picking fuzzies off his shirt.

"Ma, you're embarrassing me," Lamar muttered.

Gill, Alfonzo, and Isabel approached the group, each of them watching Oscar closely as they moved around him. He stared back warily.

Alfonzo moved closer to Lorraine Whitmore. "My dad and Gill's parents and Matt's parents are about three blocks down on the corner of Beams Avenue if you want to join them."

"Of course we'll join them!" she said.

"My mom's out to here with Godzilla," Gill added, holding his arms in a wide circle around his stomach. "You can't miss her."

"Sounds wonderful, darling."

Matt lifted his backpack over his shoulder and stepped into the street. He looked for Pastor Ruhlen and spotted him on the pay phone, talking intently. Matt twisted his lip. They didn't need a wrench in their plans. He was about to remove his laptop when he felt a presence beside him. He jumped slightly when he saw Oscar standing there, looking down at him. Matt gulped. His eyes drifted down to the bulge in Oscar's coat. He knew it was the gun. Oscar had it with him.

"You boys are not planning on letting out our little secret to Lorraine, are you?"

Matt shrugged, trying to act as if nothing was up. "What gave you that idea?"

"I do not understand why you boys insist on meddling in my affairs," he said gruffly.

"We don't want to do this," Matt returned. "We're not your judges. But we are going to protect Lamar's mom."

Oscar opened his mouth to shoot something back, but Pastor Ruhlen jogged up, interrupting their conversation. Worry plastered his face.

"What's wrong?" Matt asked as the group gathered around.

"Dude! This is terrible!" Pastor Ruhlen exclaimed, his Chia Pet hair bobbing.

"What is it?" Ms. Whitmore asked.

"Suzie!" the youth pastor shouted. "She's got . . . *laryngitis!*"

"Oh no!"

"I can't sing a duet alone! Then it would just be a du!"

"You mean a solo," Matt said.

Pastor Ruhlen bit his lip. "Well, I guess we can still throw out candy, eh?"

"We can still dance, right?"

Pastor Ruhlen shook his head. "I guess, but we'll have a long, meaningless intro now, and . . . it just won't be the same."

"Well, we can't win with just candy throwing." Matt refused to simply let their plans go down the drain. He slowly looked at Lamar, who slowly looked at Gill, who slowly looked at Alfonzo, who slowly looked at Isabel.

No one knew quite what to say until . . .

"Okay, I'll do it," Isabel said, stepping forward.

"You'll do what?" Matt asked.

"I'll sing. I know the song inside and out. I can do it."

"You can sing too?"

Isabel just smiled.

Matt's eyebrows popped up. "You're just full of surprises."

Alfonzo leaned toward Matt. "She used to sing in the bathroom when she was little," he whispered. "In the shower, on the—"

"I get the picture," Matt interrupted, throwing up a hand.

"Aw, man!" Gill protested. "But we practiced our dance moves with *five* dancers! We can't lose Iz! What happens when we do the thing and then the other thing and then the spin and the thing? With only four dancers, it'll mess up our steps!"

Matt quickly looked at Lamar, who quickly looked at Alfonzo, who quickly looked at Isabel, who quickly looked at Gill, who looked at . . .

"Oh no! No way!" Hulk cried. "Dere is no way on eard I'm gonna—"

"Hulk!" Mr. Hooligan shouted, his voice raspy but firm.

"But Dad!"

Mr. Hooligan frowned even more than usual. A long, tense moment was broken when Hulk finally said, "All right, where do I sign up?"

"You sure?" Matt asked Pastor Ruhlen. "He's wearing a gray T-shirt and jeans . . . and he can't dance."

Hulk huffed.

"I can teach you!" Gill offered. "It's cool! You just do this thing followed by another thing and then the spin and the thing!"

"How hard can dat be?" Hulk asked.

"Well," Matt admitted, "you'll definitely make our float more exciting . . ."

8

Not Another False Alarm

Like a procession of snails, the parade moved along at a crawl. Matt, Gill, Lamar, Alfonzo, Isabel, Hulk, and Pastor Ruhlen sat impatiently atop their float, waiting to get far enough down the street to see *anyone* at all. As Matt sat beneath the towering tidal wave, he was convinced they looked more like a surfer club than a church group. Pastor Ruhlen said they were attraction number ten of twenty-six in the parade, which was filled with floats, marching bands, rare cars, and other anomalies.

Directly in front of them was a walking mime studio, bustling with twenty-five silent artists. Preceding the mimes was the token loud and obnoxious "clowns-in-go-carts" feature, who followed last year's winner: the Wiz Plumbing Company float, led by the Enisburg High School marching band. This year Mr. Wiz had a whole entourage of *Wizard of Oz* characters promoting his plumbing business.

Pastor Ruhlen and Isabel were actively discussing the song they were about to sing. Gill was rushing Hulk through the CliffsNotes version of their dance moves. Matt could already tell *that* was a lost cause. But the distractions gave him the time he needed.

Matt slipped over to the makeshift sound booth and placed his laptop beside the soundboard. He flipped open the lid and got it ready. It blended quite well with the sound equipment, not looking out of place at all. Lamar nodded at Matt. They were ready. All they had to do was win the contest, and they would have the opportunity to expose Oscar safely— yet boldly enough for Lamar's mother to see. Matt took a deep breath and released it slowly. *Yeah, that's all we have to do.*

Ten minutes later, as they finally forged their way into a cheering crowd, Matt hauled four pails of candy, one after another, to the four corners of the stage. The boys took turns chucking candy into the crowd, challenging each other to see who could throw the farthest. Hulk wasn't much into giving out the sweets; he preferred to eat them. That is, until a couple of little boys in the crowd called him a pig— at the top of their lungs. *Then* Hulk got the spirit. He started whipping fistfuls of candy into the crowd, guffawing every time he hit someone in the head. *A great attraction,* Matt thought, *for a church float.*

"Come to Enisburg Community Church and learn about walking in love. Now take this!" Whump!

"Psst . . . Matt!" Lamar whispered at one point. "Can't we make this more exciting? We have to win, remember? We have to save my mom!"

"We're just getting started," Matt assured his friend. "We typed it into the laptop. It'll happen. Just wait until our act starts."

Once their float was well into the crowd, Pastor Ruhlen said it was time, and the boys quickly took their places. Pastor Ruhlen zipped back to the sound box, nearly giddy, and cued up the CD.

"Ready, guys?" he asked giving a thumbs-up.

The boys and Isabel returned his thumbs-up.

Pastor Ruhlen ran back to the group and took his place beside Isabel. He grabbed a micro-phone. Matt, Lamar, Gill, Alfonzo, and Hulk turned their backs to them, as they had practiced. Hulk said, "This is stupid," more than once, but they just shushed him and waited for the song to start. Matt glanced over his shoulder at Isabel. She was squeezing and releasing her fist at her side.

"I'm a little nervous," Lamar whispered.

"I'm not," Hulk said.

"You ought to be," Gill told him. "You still don't know the moves!"

"Sure I do," Hulk retorted. "Da ding and da spin and da ding."

Gill huffed. "This is going to be a disaster. Look, if you want to back out, we'll understand."

"Too late," Hulk replied. "I'm in dis for da long haul. At least till noon."

The music started, a soft instrumental, slow and steady. The boys fixed themselves in place. Pastor Ruhlen began singing,

Search me . . . search me . . .
Father, search the depths of my heart.
Test who I am inside,
In the place where I am set apart.

A short bridge played and then it was Isabel's turn. Matt smiled as he waited to hear her voice. But then . . . it barely came out.

Search m . . . search m . . .

Matt leaned toward Alfonzo. "Should I help her out with the laptop?" he whispered.

Lamar, on Matt's other side, pushed him. "Yes! We have to win this!"

Matt took a step toward the sound booth and then froze. Isabel's voice returned on the second line.

Search me ... search me ...
Father, search the depths of my heart.
Hear my worries, my prayers,
The secrets I won't let depart.

Matt didn't mean to; he involuntarily whirled around. His mouth dropped open. Isabel saw him and blushed, then stared at the ground. Matt was speechless. Her voice was like an angel's.

Lamar forced Matt to turn around. "What are you doing?"

"It's like ... newly spun honey," Matt muttered.

Lamar shook his head. "I really don't want to know."

Together Pastor Ruhlen and Isabel sang,

Lord, be the Judge
Of my words and all I do.
Lead me in Your higher ways
That all may worship You.

Then *booom-ba-da-boom-ba-da-boom-boom-boom!*

That was their cue! The boys broke the soft moment with a right hand cross, left hand cross, clap, clap, stomp, stomp, spin—all at the same time. Hulk, in the middle, did his own thing, but somehow it worked. It actually worked!

"I didn't know you had it in you!" Alfonzo shouted to Hulk. "Guess we shoulda believed you!"

"Told ya!" Hulk shouted. The big lug spun around, wiggling his rear end, which Matt was sure would lose them votes.

Pastor Ruhlen and Isabel laughed hysterically with the crowd as the boys performed for two minutes solid. Each time they spun, their synchronization weakened. By the time a minute had passed, they were *all* pretty much doing their own thing.

"It's a surfin' party!" Pastor Ruhlen shouted.

And at once the song ended. The crowd laughed and clapped enthusiastically. Matt, Lamar, Gill, Alfonzo, Isabel, Hulk, and Pastor Ruhlen bowed. Matt turned and spotted his parents, Gill's parents, Lamar's mom, Oscar, and Mr. Zarza in the crowd, cheering them on. Lamar's mom was taking pictures, of course.

"Is that it?" Lamar asked Matt, sounding slightly worried.

"Not a chance," Matt replied. "This time I outlined a plot."

As the group bowed and threw more candy, Matt ran back to the laptop. They would soon start their number again for another part of the crowd; Matt thought he'd spice up their act. He typed,

> The QoolQuad delivers a perfectly
> orchestrated performance.

Then he added,

> And Hulk dances unbelievably.

Matt hit the clock key, watching to make sure the laptop went to work. He closed the lid just as Pastor Ruhlen popped up behind the sound box.

"Hey, Matt! Ready to go again?"

"More than ever," Matt said with a smile.

He jogged back to the base of the tidal wave and joined his friends, who were already in formation.

"Ya hear everyone clap for me, Calhan?" Hulk boasted.

"Yeah," Matt said. "You were ... something."

Alfonzo laughed.

As they started the song for the second time and Pastor Ruhlen sang his introduction, Matt closed his eyes and listened.

Search me ... search me ...
Father, search the depths of my heart.
Test who I am inside,
In the place where I am set apart.

And then the angel . . .

Search me . . . search me . . .
Father, search the depths of my heart.
Hear my worries, my prayers,
The secrets I won't let depart.

And then together . . .

Lord, be the Judge
Of my words and all I do.
Lead me in Your higher ways
That all may worship You.

Matt found himself praying: *Lord, you know Oscar's heart. Expose it for what it is.*

Booom-ba-da-boom-ba-da-boom-boom-boom!

Right hand cross, left hand cross, clap, clap, stomp, stomp, spin—all at the same time. They were in perfect sync!

Until . . .

"Ha ha ha!" Gill dropped to the stage as if his body were made of lead. He started shaking like clothes in a washer.

Pastor Ruhlen's eyes grew big as saucers. "Wipe out!" he cried, laughing.

"Ha ha ha!" Gill laughed hysterically.

"You're ruining our act!" Lamar cried, trying to keep the dance going. Right hand cross, left hand cross . . .

Hulk kept dancing, oblivious to Gill.

"Make it stop! Make it stop!" Gill shouted, his eyes watering.

"What?" Matt cried.

Gill pointed to his stomach, where his pager was vibrating.

The crowd laughed.

"Dey love me!" Hulk cried, dancing wildly.

Matt grabbed Gill's pager and snapped it off. He ran to the side of the float and looked back into the crowd to where Gill's parents were. He saw Mrs. Gillespie sitting on the wet curb. She would have her baby this time. For sure. It wasn't just hiccups.

"It's gonna happen!" Gill turned white. "We have to help my mom! Godzilla could hurt her! Matt! Help her!"

Matt grabbed Gill's shoulders. "Gill! Listen to me!"

"What're we gonna do?" Gill cried.

Matt shook him. "Gill! Gill! Listen to me!" Matt could only imagine how crazed he must have looked, his eyes wide, staring into Gill's. "It's going to be all right!"

"But—"

"Gill! Stop running scared! You don't know what's going to happen! Stop expecting the worst! Look for the good and you'll see the truth!"

Gill stared back at Matt for a long moment. From the corner of his eye, Matt saw Lamar looking over his shoulder.

"It ... it's gonna be all right?" Gill asked, as if Matt had said something deeply profound.

"It's gonna be all right. You're going to be a brother. A *good* brother."

"I'm gonna be a brother."

"You're gonna be a *brother!* You can teach the baby stuff ... and ... and tell him jokes! I bet he'll even laugh at them!"

"I can tell him jokes!"

Matt pulled back as Gill pushed himself up.

"I'm gonna be a brother!" he repeated. Then he grabbed Matt's arm. "But ... Oscar ..."

Matt's head snapped to Lamar. Lamar ran to the edge of the float and Matt followed. They looked back at Gill's mother, still sitting on the pavement, hanging on to Mr. Gillespie's leg.

"We gotta help her," Lamar whispered.

"What about our plan?" Matt asked.

Lamar's eyes drifted to Oscar, who stood beside Lamar's mother, frowning at Mrs. Gillespie.

"We gotta help her," Lamar repeated. "It's more important right now."

Gill ran up behind Matt, nearly knocking him off the float. "I'm gonna have a brother!" he shouted. "My mom's having a baby!"

"I knew you'd be excited," Matt said.

Pastor Ruhlen, Alfonzo, and Isabel all ran up behind Gill.

"She's having a baby *now?*" Isabel exclaimed.

"Yes!"

Pastor Ruhlen's eyes grew wide. "Dude! Where is she?"

"Back there!" Matt cried, pointing back into the crowd.

"We have to help my little buddy!" Gill yelled.

"Your *little buddy?* You sound like the Skipper!"

"Dude! This is a happenin' of colossal proportions!"

"The colossalist!" Gill shouted. Then he yelled, "I'm comin', little buddy!"

Hulk just kept dancing, ignoring them all.

"We have to get her to the hospital!" Alfonzo said, throwing his leg over the side of the float.

"What are *you* gonna do?" Matt cried.

"*You'll* think of something!" Alfonzo exclaimed with a wink.

"I'm right behind ya," Lamar said to Alfonzo.

"I'm helping, too!" Isabel followed her brother and Lamar down the side of the float.

"Gill!" Pastor Ruhlen ordered. "Get on the microphone. I'll get in the driver's seat with Hulk's dad and get him to put the pedal to the metal!" Pastor Ruhlen jumped off the side of the float like Batman into a dark alley. He ran up to the truck pulling the float and jumped in, pushing Mr. Hooligan aside. He immediately leaned on the horn, causing the parade to split like a cheap pair of pants.

Matt ran to the laptop.

Gill grabbed a microphone. "My mom's having a *baby!*" he shouted.

The crowd cheered.

"No!" Gill clarified. "I mean *right now!* She needs to get through to the hospital!"

Matt rubbed his hands together. He closed his eyes and tried to block out the chaos. He placed his fingers on the home row of his keyboard and typed,

```
Immediately emergency vehicles rushed in
to pick up Gill's mom.
```

Then suddenly, just as Matt was about to hit the clock key, he felt his stomach tighten. Hulk was within eyesight—and might be watching what he was doing. He looked at Hulk. And laughed. Hulk was oblivious to *everyone*, still dancing and whirling to the beat of his own drum. It was truly unbelievable.

Matt smacked the clock key.

Brrrrrrrrrrr! Immediately the clowns-in-carts changed course and, in formation, sped through the mimes, throwing the silent souls into silent turmoil. Mimes scattered *everywhere* as the growling vehicles cruised around their feet, dodging them by mere inches. Pastor Ruhlen and Hulk's dad honked the horn and revved the engine, causing multicolored clowns and black-and-white mimes to create swirling patterns on the pavement.

"She's back there!" Gill shouted into the microphone.

Lamar, Alfonzo, Isabel, and all the parents jumped up and down, waving their hands. The clowns spotted the crew—it was pretty hard not to—and raced right over.

"Help my little buddy!" Gill pleaded.

"Emergency vehicles," Matt muttered, staring at his laptop. He typed,

```
The clowns stopped clowning around and
swiftly helped Mrs. Gillespie and
friends on their way.
```

The clowns came to a screeching halt in front of Mrs. Gillespie. The one closest to her screamed, "She's having a baby!"

"We know!" everyone around him screamed back.

Alfonzo said something to the clowns and they formed a straight line. One cart with a sidecar shot to the front.

"Yes!" Gill shouted into the microphone.

Isabel and Alfonzo helped Mrs. Gillespie into the sidecar and then the clown sped away. Mr. Gillespie jumped onto the clown's lap in the second cart, followed by Lamar and Alfonzo, who jumped into the next two carts. Seconds later the clowns-in-carts were off. Matt stumbled and almost fell over as Pastor Ruhlen smashed the gas pedal to the floor and their float jerked forward. He suddenly wondered if the tidal wave might fall on him, but it stayed steady.

The carts hosting Gill's parents pulled in behind Pastor Ruhlen's float, trusting he had the best chance of clearing the road fast. Matt could hear Lamar and Alfonzo yelling instructions to the clowns in their carts to pull ahead and chase out the mimes, who never verbally protested. With the mimes clear, Pastor Ruhlen blared the horn as they pulled ahead, paving the way to the Enisburg Hospital. Everything was clear for a few moments, until . . .

"Munchkins!" Matt shouted.

"Move it, Munchkins!" Gill yelled into the microphone. Twenty pint-sized Munchkins, who were dancing around the Wiz Plumbing Company float, screamed as the go-carts and threatening tidal wave approached. Like ants, they fled in twenty different directions. The rest of the cast followed suit. The lion jumped out of the way, the tin man seemed less than enthusi- astic, and the scarecrow atop their float did the dumbest thing imaginable: he ran right into the house in the center of the float. Literally. It capsized and fell on someone. Two green feet underneath wiggled for help.

With the Wiz out of the way, the kids in the high school band looked surprised to see the approaching entourage. At once the tuba players blew the cheerleaders out of the way. The baton twirlers spun aside. The drummers pounded the pavement as fast as they could.

The road cleared quickly and a path was opened all the way to the hospital.

Four turns and a screeching halt later, Pastor Ruhlen stopped the giant wave in front of Enisburg Hospital, the clowns-in-carts whirring before and behind him. Nurses rushed out and helped Mrs. Gillespie exit the sidecar and get into a wheelchair.

Gill ran to the side of the float, then stopped. He turned around and ran back to Matt. Putting his hands on Matt's shoulders, he said, "Thank you."

Matt smiled. "It's the least I could do for your mom."

"No," Gill said. "I mean thank you for helping *me*. I'm gonna be a *brother!*"

Matt's smile grew wider. A warm feeling rushed through his body. "Just remember me when you're rich and famous."

Gill laughed. Then he ran to the side of the float, hopped off, and joined his parents inside the hospital.

Matt, Lamar, Alfonzo, Isabel, Hulk, all their parents, Oscar, and Pastor Ruhlen gathered at the foot of the float in front of the hospital as the clowns-in-carts sped off.

And then they waited.

And they waited.

And they waited some more.

Pastor Ruhlen finally said, "Why are we waitin', dudes?"

Matt's eyebrows shot up. "Gill's having a baby."

"That'd be funny," Hulk snorted.

"You know what I mean," Matt retorted.

"You know what I think?" Pastor Ruhlen said. "I think Gill would want us to win this parade."

Lamar blinked. "You mean, you think we should try to get back in?"

"How hard would it be?" Pastor Ruhlen asked Mr. Hooligan.

"I can detour us back through Decker Street," Hulk's dad said without enthusiasm. "We might be able to jump right back in where we came out—just a couple blocks later."

Matt looked at Lamar. Lamar looked at Alfonzo.

"But we lost Gill," Alfonzo said. "Who'll dance for him?"

"I can take the place of two people," Hulk blurted out.

"That's the truth!" Pastor Ruhlen exclaimed. "So we're still on?"

Matt's smile spread to his friends' faces. They collectively turned their heads to Oscar.

"Yes, we're still on," Matt said, trying not to let his double meaning sound too thick.

Pastor Ruhlen leaped in the air. "Whoo-hoo! Let's go!"

9

Exposed

Like a rocket, Mr. Hooligan shot them through the city streets, trying to catch up with the parade. Cars pulled aside as the giant wave cruised through one avenue after another. Matt wanted to use his laptop, but there were too many people around. The crew held on tightly as they cornered onto Decker Street. Just as Hulk's dad had anticipated, it was the perfect entrance. They put on the brakes as the wounded Wiz Plumbing Company float passed in front of them. Mr. Hooligan honked the horn and Pastor Ruhlen shouted, "Move aside, please!" into the microphone. The crowd parted and a couple police officers slid aside a barricade. The clowns-in-carts waved as they passed, as did the mimes. Quite a few members seemed to be missing from both groups— casualties of the surf. When the break opened, Mr. Hooligan hit the gas and they shot back into the parade. The crowd cheered at the surprise arrival.

Pastor Ruhlen started the CD. He and Isabel sang another encore and the boys danced . . . as did all their parents. Even Oscar reluctantly joined as the boys watched him out of the corners of their eyes. Hulk definitely danced enough to take Gill's place. When Matt saw his own mother and father bumping hips, he put his hands over his face.

They continued their act for quite a while longer until they reached the final lap of the parade. When they passed the last barricade, they pulled into their assigned parking space and waited for the rest of the floats and attractions to arrive. A crowd of several hundred formed around a small stage that was decorated with radio station and soft drink advertisements and had speakers facing all directions.

As they waited, Matt, Lamar, Alfonzo, and Isabel nervously kept their eyes on Oscar, eager to see him forced to come clean.

"Ladies and gentlemen! May I have your attention, please!"

Matt and his friends whirled around. The mayor of Enisburg was tapping the microphone. He was a plump man with a mustache and brown suspenders. The kids and their parents gathered around.

"This is a most joyous occasion!" the mayor exclaimed. "Quite different than the parade we all expected. As you all know, we have a tradition. We have a prize to award!"

The crowd cheered.

"And this year, for the first time in Enisburg history, the judges are unanimous! This year there is only *one* float that could truly be considered the most exciting."

The crowd laughed. Matt, his family, and his friends nervously awaited the announcement.

"For an excellent—and perfectly orchestrated—performance . . . Mick Ruhlen, are you out there somewhere?"

The crowd cheered as Pastor Ruhlen's face lit up. "Right-e-o!" With a skip and a jump, he pushed his way up to the stage and took his place beside the mayor. He slung his arm around the mayor as though they were old friends. Matt was pretty sure they'd never met.

Matt looked at Lamar. Lamar looked at Matt. Yes! *Time to write!*

Matt excused himself and cut back to their float. He climbed up the rear, made his way to the sound box, and fired up his laptop. As it booted, Matt listened to Pastor Ruhlen's acceptance speech.

"Well, I just want you to know this is super-nif in all respects. And anytime you wanna surf on down to Enisburg Community Church, we'd be ecstatically enthusiastic to have y'all visit!" He accepted a plaque from the mayor and shook his hand.

The mayor made an offhand comment about how he was glad they had decided to come back and join the parade. Pastor Ruhlen concurred. He was about to walk away when Matt opened his word processor and quickly typed,

```
Pastor Ruhlen calls up Oscar for
helping. And soon the treachery is
revealed!
```

Matt hit the clock key and at once the mayor suggested, "Mick, you couldn't have done this all by yourself! Why don't you bring up your crew!"

The crowd laughed.

Pastor Ruhlen laughed, too. "Yah! What was I thinkin'? Boys! Isabel! Get up here!"

Seeing Lamar look back at him, Matt threw his hands up in the air. He hadn't expected *that*. Matt twisted his lip. *Misunderstandings.* He should have been more clear. Pastor Ruhlen motioned toward the boys and Isabel. Swiftly Matt typed,

```
Oscar's true intention--his secret--is
exposed! And so is his gun! For the
world to see!
```

He hit the clock key. The icon changed and put things into motion. Matt let out a short breath and closed his laptop. He hid it under the sound booth. Then he climbed down, pushed his way through the crowd, and joined his friends onstage.

Pastor Ruhlen had a big, cheesy smile on his face. He pointed to each of the friends, introducing them.

"This is Lamar, Matt, Alfonzo, Isabel, and—"

Hulk grabbed the microphone. "Hulk Hooligan! Da name is Hulk Hooligan! How many o' ya liked my dancin'?"

Many members of the crowd cheered.

"Autographs afterward!" Hulk shouted.

The crowd laughed.

Pastor Ruhlen laughed. "Yeah, okay, he's not very timid. And our last member, Gill, is in the hospital. He's a bit busy right now. He's having a baby."

The crowd laughed again. Hulk snickered again.

"In fact, can we have all the parents and Oscar come up here? They were with us during the last part of the parade."

Finally!

Matt exchanged glances with each of his friends. They stepped back and let their parents through. Pastor Ruhlen introduced Matt's mom and dad, Alfonzo's dad, Mr. Hooligan, Nate, and Lamar's mom. Then he said, "And this is Oscar

Brown. He financed our float this year. Let's hear it for Oscar!"

The spectators clapped their hands.

Lorraine Whitmore stood back and took a picture.

Oscar waved. And as he did, Matt spotted the shiny gun handle in his jacket pocket. Matt tightened his lips, muttering a prayer.

Oscar put his arm down and stepped back. Then he headed for the end of the stage.

He was walking away.

Wide-eyed, Matt looked at Lamar. Lamar turned to Alfonzo, who promptly stuck out his foot. Oscar's shoe caught on Alfonzo's and Oscar lost his footing. He hit the stage with a crash.

"Oh! Sorry!"

When Oscar hit, his jacket popped open and at once his gun shot out, flying across the stage. It slid to a stop at the mayor's feet.

The mayor gasped.

The parents gasped.

Even Hulk gasped.

When the mayor picked up the gun, murmurs ran through the crowd. A few women screamed. Lamar's mother stood in silence, her hand over her mouth.

"What is the meaning of this?" the mayor demanded, inspecting the weapon. Then his eyes narrowed as Oscar stood. "Hey . . . don't I know you from somewhere?"

Panic hit Oscar's face and he quickly looked back at Lorraine. He peered out at the crowd, then back at the mayor.

"Oscar . . . ," Lorraine Whitmore whispered.

"Go ahead, tell him," Alfonzo said.

"No more secrets," Lamar said boldly.

"Well?" the mayor demanded.

Oscar looked at Lorraine and let out a sigh.

"Tell her." Lamar grabbed his mother's hand. "Tell her about the lie you've been living. Tell her about the gun. Tell her about the—"

"I know where I've seen you!" the mayor shouted. "You're the Crowley Mobster!"

Lorraine Whitmore's mouth dropped open.

"He's been lying to you, Ma," Lamar said. "He hasn't been working at the office on Friday nights at all. I told you."

Lorraine Whitmore's eyes filled with tears. They shifted to Lamar and back to Oscar. "Is . . . is that true? You're a . . . a . . ."

"A *great* actor!" the mayor shouted. "When this guy played the Crowley Mobster, I was on the edge of my seat!"

Matt blinked.

Lamar blinked.

Alfonzo and Isabel blinked.

"Actor?" Matt said.

"Actor?" Lamar said.

"Actor?" Alfonzo and Isabel said.

"Yes!" the mayor cried again. "He's in *The Street Men*, right?" The mayor punched the air. "No alarm folks," he said into the microphone. "He plays a gangster in the new play down at the Playhouse. Just a plastic gun!" The mayor squeezed the trigger a few times and the crowd chuckled. He slapped the gun into Oscar's hand and then started talking to the crowd again, relaying one announcement after another. Matt and everyone in his group slowly moved to the back of the stage, dumbfounded.

Matt stared at the ground in disbelief.

Lamar couldn't take his eyes off Oscar.

Alfonzo and Isabel scratched their heads.

Oscar shrugged. "I wanted it to be a surprise when I invited you to a performance," he said to Lorraine. "Still working out the kinks." He shoved the gun into his pocket. "I have been carrying this thing around with me all week to practice my draw. I am not very good." He tried to pull it out but it got stuck. "See?" Then he added, "Please, do not tell my brother and sister. I want to surprise *them*, anyway."

"But . . . but we *saw* you!" Lamar pushed his way forward. "At the school!"

"I know. Not one of my better practice sessions. I told you I wanted it to be a secret."

"Dis is da guy ya thought was big trouble?" Hulk said. "Duh, Whitmore. Look at 'im. He couldn't hurt a fly."

Oscar chuckled. "Of course not." Then he looked at each of the boys and Isabel. "Wait . . . Did you think . . ."

Lorraine grabbed her son's shoulder. "Oh, this explains a lot."

Matt felt a sharp pain in his stomach. He stepped backward. He could feel his head spinning. His eyes shot toward his laptop, sitting blamelessly in the distance, under the sound box on the float.

Treachery *was* revealed—true treachery, the treachery Matt and his friends had created. They'd had no right to judge Oscar. They didn't even know the facts. At all.

Sam was right. They were getting careless with the laptop.

Pastor Ruhlen was right. They were getting careless with their thoughts.

Matt was right. *Stop running scared,* he had said to Gill. *You don't know what's going to happen. Stop expecting the worst. Look for the good and you'll see the truth.* If only he could learn to live it himself instead of just preaching it to Gill.

Matt's eyes drifted up to catch Lamar's. They looked as sick and stunned as his own. *Misunderstandings*, Matt thought. *They never are as funny in real life as they are in the sitcoms.*

"We're sorry," Matt said, his voice barely escaping. "*I'm* sorry. After seeing the gun and your performance and then the cash . . . well, I guess I expected that you're something you're not."

Oscar nodded, putting his hand on Matt's shoulder. "I really am a loan officer, that is all," he assured them. "Well, and an actor-wannabe who gets paid by the performance."

Matt was reeling. Oscar wasn't the only actor. Matt and his friends had been acting, too . . . acting out of fear. They'd given in to it. And with a mob mentality, he and his friends had judged an innocent man. Matt suddenly felt as if he were drowning, his feet anchored in the cement of his own foolishness. He heard himself silently praying the words he had heard an angel sing earlier that morning. *Lord, be the Judge of my words and all I do.* Matt added, *Lord, be my Judge . . . know my thoughts and help me to not judge others.*

Lamar looked at Oscar for a long time, then offered his hand. "Will you forgive me?"

Oscar grabbed Lamar's hand and pulled him in. He didn't say another word, and neither did Matt or Lamar. They didn't need any more words. They didn't need any more misunderstandings. Judgment was best left to the One who had the right to judge ... and no one else.

Epilogue

It's a boy!" Gill shouted, bursting into Matt's room.

"Yes!" Matt, Lamar, and Alfonzo shouted. Matt sat at his desk; Lamar and Alfonzo sat on the edge of Matt's bed. They each gave Gill a high five.

"Good thing," Lamar said. "After Isabel moved in, I was concerned the neighborhood might get overrun with girls."

"Not a chance," Matt said with a smile.

"Yeah, you guys have to come over and see him. He looks just like me."

"You were adopted," Matt said.

"Well, okay, his hair is brown and his eyes are brown, so that's different, but otherwise—"

"In other words," Lamar said, "he looks *nothing* like you."

The boys laughed.

"Hey," Gill said, "thanks again for helping at the parade. You certainly topped yourself with that story, Matt." Then he turned to Lamar. "So what happened with Oscar? Did you nab him? Did you bring that good-for-nothing criminal down?"

"He's an *actor*," Lamar said loudly.

"You mean he's not—"

"No."

Gill whistled. "Next time you guys should investigate better. If there's one thing I've learned from detective shows, it's—"

"*Enough* with the detective shows," Lamar ordered.

"Hey, serves us right for judging," Matt said.

For a moment the room was silent. Then Lamar and Alfonzo started chuckling. They'd been flipping through pictures Lamar's mom had taken the day of the parade and had come to one of Gill shouting into the microphone.

"Move it, Munchkins!" Alfonzo said.

Gill laughed. Matt looked at the picture and smiled widely.

"Oh, here's one of Isabel singing," Lamar said.

Matt snatched it out of his hand. "Very funny," Matt said flatly. The picture was a crowd shot.

Then Matt froze. "Guys . . ."

Lamar, Gill, and Alfonzo were already on the next picture.

"Guys . . ."

"What?" Lamar asked, not looking up.

Matt spun around to his desk and pulled out a magnifying glass. He held it over the photograph and then pulled away. His stomach churned. The picture was fuzzy but the image was unmistakable. A figure stood . . . watching. In a trench coat and thin cowboy boots.

"Guys! It's Sam! I can see him!"

The boys all looked at each other and then jumped up and gathered around Matt. They squinted at the fuzzy picture.

"You sure?" Alfonzo asked.

Matt nodded. "I'd know him anywhere."

"Except that doesn't look like a *him*," Gill observed.

Matt couldn't believe it. Gill was right. Sam had long blond hair . . . and though it was out of focus, the face certainly looked female.

"Sam's a . . . *Samantha?*" Lamar asked.

The room fell silent.

Pop!

The four boys whirled around when they heard the bedroom door open. Matt's dad stood in the doorway, his hands behind his back. If they had guilt written all over their faces, he didn't seem to notice. "Alfonzo, when does your dad get home?" he asked.

Alfonzo shrugged. "Maybe an hour."

Mr. Calahan nodded. "Because I was just working on remodeling your basement and I found a loose floorboard. I pulled it out."

"That's no problem," Alfonzo said. "He won't care."

Matt's dad swallowed hard. "Actually, I think he will. I found *this* underneath." He pulled his hands out from behind his back. Lying in them was a heavy, dusty bar. Of gold.

To be continued . . .

About the Author

For ten years Christopher P. N. Maselli has been sharing God's Word with kids through stories. He is the author of multiple award-winning projects, including an international children's magazine, a middle-grade adventure novel series, videos, and more.

Chris lives in Fort Worth, Texas, with his wife, Gena, and their feline twins, Zoë and Zuzu. He is actively involved in his church's *KIDS Church* program, and his hobbies include inline skating, collecting *It's a Wonderful Life* movie memorabilia, and "way too much" computing.

We want to hear from you. Please send your comments about this book to us in care of the address below. Thank you.

Zonder**kidz**®

Grand Rapids, MI 49530
www.zonderkidz.com